# Delta q

The delta q of the title refers to the uncertainty or inexactness in the measurement of the position of a particle. According to the Heisenberg Uncertainty Principle, the product of $\Delta q$ and $\Delta p$, the uncertainty in the momentum of the particle, cannot be less than Planck's constant, $h = 6.63 \times 10^{-27}$ erg seconds. In effect, the Uncertainty Principle postulates an experimentally verifiable limit to the accuracy with which one can observe and describe the universe. Science thus supports something that most writers have long suspected: there is a limit to man's knowledge.

A. Truman Schwartz

# Delta q

## Stories by
## Alvin Greenberg

University of Missouri Press
Columbia & London
1983

Copyright © 1983 by Alvin Greenberg
University of Missouri Press, Columbia, Missouri 65211
Library of Congress Catalog Card Number 82–20075
Printed and bound in the United States of America

Library of Congress Cataloging in Publication Data

Greenberg, Alvin.
  Delta q : stories.

  (AWP ; 5)
  I. Title. II. Series: AWP (Series); 5.
PS3557.R377D4     1983       813'.54       82–20075
ISBN 0–8262–0397–3

Some of the stories in this collection appeared originally in the following magazines:

  *Antaeus* ("The Serious World and Its Environs")
  *Antioch Review* ("Delta q" and "The Ascent of Man")
  *Descant* ("Disorder and Belated Sorrow")
  *Eureka Review* ("Leanings")
  *Mississippi Review* ("Game Time," "To Be or Not To Be," and "Not
    a Story by Isaac Bashevis Singer")
  *Quarterly West* ("The State of the Art")
  *Story Quarterly* ("The Power of Language")

for Skip

# The AWP Award Series in Short Fiction

This volume is the first-place winner of the fifth annual AWP Award Series in Short Fiction, sponsored by Associated Writing Programs, an organization of over ninety colleges and universities with strong curricular commitments to the teaching of creative writing, headquartered at Old Dominion University, Norfolk, Virginia.

Each year, a collection of outstanding short fiction is selected by a panel of distinguished fiction writers from among the many submitted to the AWP Award Series competition. The University of Missouri Press is proud to be associated with the series and to present *Delta q* as this year's selection.

# Contents

# I. Momentum

# The Power of Language

i.

No one left on the island any longer except me and the feral pigs, so you can imagine my surprise when I was out walking the main road down the center of the island this morning and found the word LOVE written in the dirt. I would not have thought the pigs were familiar with such a word, let alone able to spell it correctly. The letters, gouged deep in the sandy roadbed and stretching large, from one side of the road to the other, looked at first like the usual markings left by the pigs in their regular foraging as they root up the earth for mast, which was why I failed to notice anything out of the ordinary right off and simply kept on along my morning stroll. I must have gone on another hundred yards or so before I suddenly realized I had seen something quite remarkable. I quickly retraced my steps.

By the time I got back to the house, quite certain after a careful examination of the markings in the road that I had indeed seen what I had seen, it occurred to me that there were, of course, at least two other possible explanations for this phenomenon. But I was positive, first of all, that for some months now there had not been another human being on the island besides myself. There had never been many of us here to begin with: a few visitors like myself, come to work in the big house for the sake of the privacy this island retreat offered, and a dozen or so permanent residents, the ones who made it possible for the rest of us to stay and work here. And the visitors, myself excepted, had all been whisked away to the mainland by boat within days of the time it was realized that the island was adrift and moving slowly away from the Georgia coast and out into the Atlantic. I had some difficulty convincing them to let me stay on, but after all, there was no

3

immediate danger apparent—the island was merely drifting, not sinking; if anything, it seemed to have become lighter for having forsaken its roots and to have risen another foot or so above sea level—and other boats would soon be departing, and I did have some small influence here.

The permanent residents, naturally, stayed on somewhat longer. This was where their homes were, after all, where many of them had lived most of their lives. Where would they go now? But soon enough, within days in fact, as we all began to realize that the island was heading steadily out to sea and that the mainland was falling away on the horizon with surprising rapidity, they too agreed to leave, gathering such possessions as could easily be loaded on the two remaining boats and hurrying to the dock, for it was late afternoon already when the mass decision was made, and many were overtaken by the sudden fear that by sunrise the next day the mainland would be out of sight altogether. It was a reasonable fear, for none of them had ever been out of sight of the mainland before, and it was also reasonable that in their anxiety they should not at first have remembered that I was still on the island. No doubt the minute they realized it, even in the midst of loading the boats, they hurried back to the house, but by then I was gone, safely off by myself, wandering about the far end of the island, where they would never have time to search for me before darkness fell. All there was for them to find was my brief note, explaining my decision to remain on the island, inasmuch as such a decision, which under the circumstances was bound to seem a bit bizarre even to the most rational reader, could be explained. I was grateful when I returned to the big house the next morning—and the mainland was indeed no longer visible by then—to find that they had at least left my belongings, for I could see that someone had begun to pack my suitcase and then abandoned that task, unfinished, in the middle of the room. I also appreciated the note the Director had left, promising to return for me in a day or so, when I had had more time to reconsider my foolhardy decision. It is to his credit that he did indeed come back the following day, and that Coast Guard helicopters searched the island every few days for a couple of weeks, but thanks to his warning I had found myself a secure hiding place by then.

So I was quite certain that there was not another human being on the island who could have written that word. I had soon gone through all the small homes of the permanent residents and assured myself that no one had remained behind, though I was pleased to see that they had left their pantries well stocked. It is possible, of course, that someone else has arrived on the island since those days of exodus, but why would I not have seen such a person by now? Surely whoever it was would have come to the main house by now in search of food—for I soon moved all the supplies to the big pantry here—or shelter from the frequent rain. Surely I would have seen such a new visitor by now, even someone washed ashore from a shipwreck or someone who had put into one of the coves in a small boat, for I wander the island from end to end, walk the beaches, explore all its inner recesses, and I have never yet seen another footprint but my own. And this is no place for small boats any longer, for the island rides the high seas now.

No, there is no one else but me on this island now, of that I am quite sure, and I confine my writing solely to these sheets of white paper and I do my writing solely on this small portable typewriter that I brought with me to work on. And if I were to take to scrawling letters in the sand, I do not think I would have written what I found written there. But it did occur to me, of course, that there was another possible explanation: namely, that the combination of those four letters in the sand, into that one word that I read there, was merely fortuitous, a chance conglomeration of accidental lines gouged in the road by the pigs in their ordinary search for food, as meaningless as any of the irregular markings they leave scattered across the forest floor, however many of them seem vaguely to resemble an $X$ or a $T$ or a $V$ or an $L$. All through the daylight hours the pigs course the island, pushing their snouts through the sandy soil in their hunger for roots and acorns, and, as many pigs as there are here, for they breed

5

freely, untroubled by natural enemies and held in check only by the island's limited food supply, it was inevitable that some of their scratchings in the earth should, purely by chance, look not unlike some of the scratchings we humans make.

Still, the firmness and clarity of those letters seems convincing to me, the *O* in particular, nearly perfect in its roundness and therefore most unlikely to be merely the chance by-product of the search for food. And the *E*, what about the *E*, could you really expect a complex letter like that *E* to occur just by accident? And then of course the biggest question of all, the question of the whole word itself, what were the odds on that? There is, of course, the old gang-of-monkeys explanation, and I suppose that cannot entirely be put aside. But as I recall, the monkeys in that theory are always given typewriters to work on; they do not actually have to make the letters, only to strike the keys and let the words take their accidental shapes, to let some of the ready-made letters fall by chance into the patterns we call words, as eventually some would do. That is just a matter of statistical theory, in fact, but what has happened here is not theory at all, it is not statistics, there was no bunch of non-word conglomerations of letters, false starts as it were, with here or there an actual word occurring in their midst; here there was just a single word, just a single reality: LOVE.

ii.

I am fairly certain that I know now which pig is teaching them to write. Twice already, in the week since I first saw that word in the road, I have come across sizable groups of pigs engaged in what appear to be very unusual activities, for pigs at least, and she seemed to be the focus of their attention on both occasions. The first time was the very next day after I had spotted that word. I had gone down the main road where I had seen it, late in the morning again, wanting another look at the word, because in the course of thinking about it and trying to set down these few words of my own about it when I came back to the house the previous day, it had all begun to seem very unreal. It was no surprise to me, however, to find that no trace of the word remained. I seemed to remember that once, when I awoke in the middle of the night, I had heard it raining, and that alone would have been enough to wipe any sign of the previous day's activity off the sandy roadway. Yes, I am certain it must have rained the night before. I do not believe, though, that I would have found the word there even if I had returned at once, that very afternoon I discovered it. No, I think the pigs would have been back there before me, rooting up the evidence of their literacy as effectively as they rooted up nuts and mold, scattering with their tiny, sharp hooves the message they had written in the sand. For subsequent events have led me to conclude that the pigs do not want me to know that they are learning to read and write. And given the history of relationships between pigs and humans, who can blame them?

But I do know. When I passed the spot where they had left their word on the road the day before and found nothing remained, I kept on along the road for another mile or so, watching the road for signs, certain that sooner or later I would find some confirmation of my remarkable discovery of the preceding day. Then I turned off on a seldom-used side road, overgrown with young palmettos and crisscrossed by the rotting trunks of fallen palms. Soon the road passed into a heavy stand of thick-trunked live oaks, some of the oldest on the island I believe, some of them perhaps several hundred years old, possibly dating back to a time before there were even pigs on the island. It was there that I saw them, grouped in a clearing in the midst of the giant oaks and partially concealed from view by the heavy, gray-green curtains of Spanish moss that hung from the branches of the oaks. Even hidden as they were, however, so that I could not count them, I realized that I saw there more pigs by far than I had ever, in all my wanderings, seen gathered in one place at one time on this island. Normally, you never saw more than a few at one time, or at the most a sow with half a dozen piglets nosing about in the underbrush in her vicinity, and maybe one or two other adult pigs nearby. But here there must have been several dozen, and they were not feeding; they were, so far as I could tell, simply standing there. Not for long, of course. I had stepped off the road and hidden myself behind a tree the moment I spotted them, but it was a young red pine, not really thick enough in the trunk to conceal me, and no doubt the pigs had heard me coming as well. It would not surprise me to learn that they had a lookout posted back up the road. So they quickly broke ranks and scattered, as they always did when you came upon them, squealing away into the under-brush with a speed you never quite expected of them.

But not before I noticed a number of things in that strange, brief moment of silence when I first came upon them, begin-ning with the fact that they were not feeding, that I had never seen even a small group of pigs just standing there like that. In addition, it seemed, though I could not tell for certain be-cause of the trees and hanging moss that interrupted my view, that they were not just randomly standing there but that they were gathered in some kind of order. Not in rows, exactly, but it seemed quite clear that there was some sort of order in their gathering, in spite of the fact that the group consisted of an inordinate number of young ones. Oh, there are always plenty of piglets on the island, two or three or even half a dozen to a sow, but here I think the ratio must have been more on the order of ten to one. Yes, I thought at once, get them started young, that's always the best way. And they were so attentive, at least for that moment before they broke ranks and scattered in all directions, away from me, that it took some time more, long after they had all fled and the forest around me was left silent and empty once again, before I realized that I had been watching them so closely that I had almost missed seeing what their attention was focused on. But I had not missed her. I might have seen her only at the last moment and out of the corner of my eye, but so striking was her presence that long after they had all gone, when I had come out from behind the small pine to stand in the middle of the road and think about all I had just witnessed, I retained a clear and vivid image of her.

Not only did her height make her stand out above all the others gathered before her, but it suddenly occurred to me

8

that in seeing her I had also seen something even more un-usual. For in the few seconds I had had to observe her, I had seen her take a step or two forward, and as she did so, the pig standing in front of her backed away. And I realized that never in my life, either here among the wild pigs on this is-land or among the domestic pigs on farms I had visited in the past, had I ever seen a pig back up. It is simply a thing that pigs do not do, nor do most other animals, naturally, so far as I know. Humans excepted. You can train a horse or a dog, or even a bear, to backstep, of course, but they do not do it naturally and neither do pigs. They will sidestep, they will turn about and move away, but no, they do not back up. And yet that was just what I had seen, a pig backing up.

The presence of that regal-looking sow would have done it, of course, if anything would. She was by far the tallest pig I had seen on my several visits to the island, and she was a solid, gleaming, unblemished black, of a purity that was rare, if not hitherto unknown, among the island pigs, for their an-cestry was almost as diverse as that of the American popula-tion itself. They had been brought to the island in all the wide variety of breeds that can be imagined, by French settlers and African slaves, by Spanish and English colonists, by priva-teers of various nationalities, by a long succession of deter-mined but ill-fated pig raisers from the mainland, and it is even possible that an indigenous variety of wild boar flour-ished on the island long before the Europeans arrived. But that makes little difference now, when they have all gone back to the wild, have had the run of the island for centuries, in fact, and have bred and interbred and filled the island to the limits of the pig population it can support with piglets of every size, shape, and coloration. Here and there, of course, you can see the markings of some recognizable breed—the sharply ridged spine reminiscent of the razorback or the wide, black belly band of the Poland China or the long tusks of the wild boar—but always those traits are so intermixed with others that the island appears a veritable melting pot for pigs. It is possible that they know many languages, not just English.

The second time I came across them in the midst of their

studies, they were on a little beach not more than a couple hundred yards from the house. We were all so startled by meeting—me at finding them busy at their lessons so close to the house and them, no doubt, at my venturing out of the house so early in the morning, which was only the product of the several sleepless nights that had followed my previous encounter with them in the forest—that for a long time, it may have been a full minute, none of us moved. The pigs turned, en masse, with one exception, and stared at me as I emerged through the palmettos onto the white sand. And I, for my part, had ample time to examine them as they stood there in some sort of order, though once again I would have had a difficult time defining it precisely, but all with their backs to the sea and facing the big, black sow. She alone, impressive, stolid, undisturbed, did not turn to look at me, but stood tall and unmoving instead, and kept her gaze firmly fixed on her pupils, until at last, with a slight nod of her head, she dismissed them, and once again they scattered, squealing wildly as they fled across the road and into the underbrush. As the last of them scampered off the beach, she, their teacher, their queen, turned about and followed them. She did not even glance in my direction. She looked once about the beach in front of her, where all her students had been standing attentively moments ago, and then she turned and walked away.

I hurried at once down to the beach where they had been assembled, but of course there was nothing to be seen. In their milling about before they stampeded and fled, they had naturally erased all the signs of their studies, all the words they had painstakingly scratched out in the sand, and once again I had no more solid evidence of their work than in the oak grove, where their sudden departure had so churned up the covering of leaves and debris on the forest floor as to effectively erase all traces of their writing. There was nothing left for me to do but return to the house, to my own writing, to set down these strange events I have witnessed before they come to seem so unreal that even I cannot believe what I have observed, and as a result I came upon the house itself so suddenly that I was quite startled, almost frightened, as if everything had altered and even the house itself, in my brief absence, had made some unexpected move.

iii.

The house shuddered slightly that morning when the island broke loose, but that was all. We had just sat down together at the long dining room table for breakfast, the Director and all the visitors working on the island at the time, when the whole house seemed to give an almost imperceptible twitch. A little plaster fell around the dining room, along the walls, not much. The southern coast has never been noted for earthquakes; nothing could have been less likely, in fact, except what was actually happening. And of course we did not yet know what that was, though it must have been developing for a long time, many years perhaps, and all we felt then was the final moment of breaking loose, the last deep roots of the live oaks, perhaps, relinquishing their hold on the continent and setting the island free at last from its ancient moorings. But it seemed like nothing at all at the time, and we merely glanced at each other around the table and set to passing the coffee and toast and marmalade, though we did not fail to notice that the Director excused himself at once and had still not returned by the end of the meal. He had a reputation as a great worrier, however. Breakfast over, we returned to our rooms and our work, giving little thought to this odd but apparently trivial occurrence. But by late afternoon, when I emerged from my long day's work, I found the rest of the guests assembled in small groups out on the front lawn, which reached down to the water's edge. They were remarking how the position of the neighboring island, across the channel, appeared to have changed, so that we could now see well into the sandy cove on its seaward side, which had never been visible to us before.

Out on the edges of the broad lawn, near where the forest crept in upon the perimeter of the grounds, several small groups of pigs had also gathered. But that was by no means an unusual occurrence, for they often fed on the grounds, even coming quite close to the house at times, so long as no one disturbed them. Perhaps it is only in retrospect that I see them, like us, facing the water and the island across the way. I cannot help thinking that they, so much closer in touch with their environment in all its subtle changes, already knew perfectly well what was happening. Perhaps they had known for a long time what was coming. At any rate, I am certain they stayed out there on the lawn, for a longer time and in greater numbers and in closer proximity to us than was usual, and watched, with us, the shadows deepen in the cove of the island opposite. Then they were gone, without any of us having noticed their departure. But why should we, given the surprising event that was already unfolding before us? We shivered in the wind off the sea and huddled closer in our groups, talking in whispers, and at last turned about ourselves, and in the rapidly fading light of the winter sunset crossed the lawn, all of us together, and entered the house. It was only then, as we sat down at the supper table, that the Director informed us, from the head of the table, in his calm and reassuring voice, that it appeared that our island retreat, to which we visitors had come to attend to our own work in an atmosphere of total freedom from the ordinary cares of the world, was now itself in the process of retreating from that mainland we, too, had chosen to leave behind.

Surely no one on the island slept that night. We were gripped by a combination of fear and exaltation that few of us had ever experienced before. Hidden supplies of whiskey came suddenly to light, and the great living room that evening, where the fire blazed so high the Director was forced to warn us to restrain ourselves from piling on log after log after log, seemed torn by conflicting desires either to hold a party that roared as wildly as the fire, the orgy that had always been predicted for the eve of the apocalypse, or to huddle in the farthest, darkest corners of the room, whispering like frightened tourists besieged in a foreign country by the sudden, inexplicable outbreak of a war and praying for the success of the evacuation plans that had been announced for the following days.

I myself withdrew to my room to work. That seemed the

**The Power of Language**

most reasonable thing to do under the circumstances, for I had much still to do on the project I had brought to the island to work on, and I had not yet made my decision—no, it had not even occurred to me as a possibility yet—to remain on the island, come what may. I worked well into the night, long past my usual hours, by no means immune myself to the sense of excitement that had taken over the house, and it must have been two or three in the morning when I finally rose from my desk and, only wanting to stretch my legs a bit, wandered back to the living room. Everyone was still there. The fire had died down and the lights had all been turned off and the whole group had assembled their chairs and couches to face the giant picture window that looked out to the north, across the front lawn and the channel to where, in the light of the full moon that had now risen, the neighboring island was hardly visible any longer. An arm—in the darkness I could not tell whose—raised up from an overstuffed chair and pointed out the window to where, just barely in sight, the island's easternmost tip could still be seen, a long, low slope of beach barely distinguishable from the sea. No one spoke a word. We were moving out to sea, slowly, like a great ship. It was clear that we had set forth on a most remarkable journey. Yes, *we*, I thought. And then quite suddenly I knew that I would not abandon this voyage. Not now. No matter how they tried to make me.

Eventually even the Coast Guard gave up its search, though not for several weeks. Perhaps the island had at last drifted beyond helicopter range. Doubtless it had moved by then into international waters, beyond the province of the state of Georgia, to which it had originally been appended. Often I have sat by that very same picture window from which we watched that first night slowly fade and the sun come up on a broad and empty sea—from which I myself have since witnessed both sunrise and sunset on the same day, as the island turns about in the current and wind—and considered how even now, in all likelihood, this drifting piece of America, no great amount of land, really, being only some eight miles across at its widest point, must be creating some interesting problems in maritime law, though I see no evidence that anyone is paying the slightest attention to it. I see planes from time to time, of course, transatlantic flights I suppose, since they remain at great altitude, and no doubt there are satellites capable of tracking the island's position quite effectively. I don't imagine there will be any real problem so long as the island remains clear of major shipping lanes, unless perhaps someone attempts to claim it for salvage. Is it possible to claim an island for salvage, I wonder, an American island that has severed its ties from its nation of origin and embarked upon international waters? Does international law cover such a case as this? Aside from the house, though, there is little here I can think of that would make salvaging a profitable operation, even if it were possible for some ambitious would-be salvager to take an island in tow. But what will happen, I wonder, what sorts of claims will arise, when eventually, as no doubt it must, the island drifts in to the mainland somewhere—in North or South America, or perhaps even Africa—and runs aground against the shore of some foreign country? That could take years of course—we have the whole of the Atlantic, north and south, to drift in—and settling such a tricky and unprecedented case in international law would undoubtedly take many years more. Looking out my great window upon the wide and open sea, I cannot see that the fate of this island will be readily settled, not for a long, long time.

iv.

Until today I was beginning to fear that perhaps I had placed too much importance upon a single word, and that one a word glimpsed only briefly and by chance, written in the sand, and then seen no more. Many weeks have passed since the last time I saw the queen of the pigs guiding her subjects in their studies, though I can well understand how after those two previous encounters they might have found it necessary to remove their classes to farther corners of the island and to keep more careful lookouts posted. Centuries of sharing the island with humans and learning the danger such proximity has posed to their very lives would undoubtedly have bred a certain caution into their behavior. But now that the spring is well advanced and the weather much improved—it has grown so hot for this time of year, in fact, that I feel certain we must be drifting steadily south, into the tropics—and I find it much more comfortable to be outdoors and wandering about the island at all hours of the day, I expect to find further signs of their progressing education. Not all over the island, of course, but at least here and there, in some isolated spot where perhaps with the pride of accomplishment some piglet has trotted off, refusing to obliterate a word or a phrase transcribed with unprecedented grace and accuracy. That I have not come across any such further evidence—neither a misspelled word left behind in frustration by a struggling young scholar nor a sentence abandoned halfway through by the sudden flight of its writer as I stumbled accidentally upon the scene of creation—I can only attribute to the shrewdness of intellect for which pigs have always been known. It makes no difference, of course; the single word is quite enough. Have we not extrapolated enormous dinosaurs from a single bone, whole species from an imprint in the clay, entire civilizations from a potsherd?

Still, I always keep my eyes to the ground as I go about the island, so certain am I that further evidence of what I know is happening here will eventually come to my attention, if only I remain alert. And from time to time I stop to pick up and sample the acorns and other nuts I find on the forest floor or beside the road, for I have begun to realize that even the well-stocked pantry that was left to me here will not last indefinitely. The fact is, I am growing quite tired of canned foods. For a while I relished the fresh oysters from the tidal streams. But because the island floats now upon the ocean's surface, rising and falling with the ocean's rhythms, and because its tidal streams, having achieved a certain equilibrium, no longer cleanse themselves by emptying and filling twice a day, I cannot trust the oysters. I am glad I have not eaten pork, at least for a long time. The nuts are somewhat bitter, but very tasty on the whole. And recently I have begun to supplement my diet with mushrooms, too, having found in the extensive library at the big house an excellent, well-illustrated guide to edible mushrooms.

By midmorning today I had nearly filled an old coffee can with mushrooms, for I am still new to this diet and afraid to eat them in the forest without bringing them back to the house to check them against their pictures and descriptions in the book. I was even wondering, as I straggled along, eyes to the ground, whether the pigs themselves might not benefit from a chance to examine that particular text, and it occurred to me that I might leave it out for their perusal, on the side porch where it would be protected from rain, perhaps along with a number of other books they might find edifying. I was not sure just what, though I felt reasonably certain they might find a dictionary a valuable asset. Perhaps some scientific texts, in the more accessible, popularized vein, for I have no evidence on the state of their mathematics. Possibly one of my own books, even if only as a sign of the sort of human who shares this island with them, some indications of the workings of his mind and language, for what could a pig be expected to make of a fiction? Though only time would enable me to discover what really interested them, I was beginning to feel, as I considered how best to make my library available to them, that given sufficient time I might indeed make a considerable contribution to their education.

Just then a sudden flash of light caught my eyes, the glitter of sunlight off the glassy calm of the ocean, for I had arrived at the end of this particular road on the southwestern tip of the island—or what had originally been the southwestern tip, for I realized that today, to catch the sun like that, it must have swung far around toward the east—and would have to retrace my steps now. I had taken my shirt off some ways back and tied it about my waist, for it was the hottest day I had experienced on the island so far, and an almost visible humidity hung heavily in the forest air; my pants were rolled to my knees, and my shoes, too, I had removed some time back, not very far from the house, and left by the side of the road, with my socks stuffed inside them. I would have kept them on, I suppose, to walk in the forest itself, where the ground was littered with sharp-edged pine cones and broken twigs, but here on the road I enjoyed the feel of the warm sand on my bare feet. I watched the sand sift between my toes as I walked, watched for nuts and mushrooms along the sides of the road, watched, above all, for any significant-looking markings along the way, and so kept my eyes totally focused on the ground before and around me that I did not see her till I was almost right on top of her.

She stood squarely in the center of the road before me, the glossy black of her skin shimmering as brightly as the sea and everything about her size and stance and posture speaking of authority. Where she stood, she effectively blocked my route home, for on one side the road was bounded by swamp and on the other by a stretch of pine forest that I dared not risk in bare feet. But I did not want to move away from her or try to get around her; in fact, I am not sure that I could have pulled myself away if I had wanted to, so entranced was I by the power of her presence. She gave an enormous sense of strength as she stood there, quite motionless, head lowered and eyes, piercing black eyes, fixed directly upon me. And not ten feet away! I could easily understand the authority she held over the other pigs on the island and could just as easily have knelt in the sandy road in front of her and submitted myself to whatever lessons she had in mind for me, except I did not get the sense that that was what she wanted of me. She was simply assessing me—I am sure that was all there was to it—as I stood uncertainly in the middle of the road, clutching my coffee can full of mushrooms, my body gleaming with sweat, my eyes looking back into hers as she held me transfixed. Perhaps there was nothing quite so intentional in her behavior as I believed; perhaps she had merely been leading a group of schoolchildren down to the small beach at the end of the road for their morning lesson and had come upon me, as I started back, quite by accident and only then decided to explore this encounter more fully, sending the others off to wait unseen in the darkness of the forest. But clearly she knew how to use the moment. I heard an airplane going over, high, high above, just a faint sound trailing across the silence of the island. I knew what it was and for just a second wanted to look up and search the skies for it, as I always did when I heard one passing over, but I couldn't seem to free myself to raise my head and, instead, found myself dropping my eyes to the ground. Then I heard her make a slight scuffling sound and looked quickly back up—not as quickly as I would have liked, for my neck felt stiff and uncomfortable when I tried to raise my head, and I had to settle for simply rolling my eyes up at her—to see her scraping in the sand with her left forefoot. Now, I thought, elated, now is the moment! She has something to say to me, something to show me, and now is the time, now she will show me her command of the language. But instead, as I looked at her, as I leaned toward her, waiting, anticipating, she simply pawed the earth once more with her forefoot, as if to erase the message she had begun there, and turned about and trotted regally off. I could see, as she moved away from me, her head low slung and no longer in view, the powerful thrust of her shoulders and haunches, the imperial determination in her stride, and I could not help admiring the way she had almost spoken to me and then held back at just the last moment, with a sense of restraint, as if it were not becoming of her to do so, not just yet anyway. Once, just before I lost sight of her, she paused in the road and turned and glanced over her shoulder at me. Then she hurried out of sight, off the road, among the young palmettos, and I myself trotted down the road after her, clutching the can of mushrooms to my chest, my head swaying loosely back and forth as I scanned the ground before me.

v.

Like all the islands I have ever been on, this one, too, is shaped like one of the internal organs of the human body. The question is, which? The big house is full of maps of the island; they hang in every room and range from seventeenth-century, hand-drawn maps to recent Coast Guard aerial surveys. I remember standing in front of one of these maps, a good many months ago now, the large-scale map in the hall-way, I believe, the one with details of water depth and ground elevation densely marked all over, and commenting to the Director, who happened to be passing by at that moment, that it must have often been pointed out to him that the is-land had the shape of the human heart.

"Why, no," he said, pausing to stare very hard, first at the map and then at me, as if he were seeing both of us for the first time, "no, no one has ever mentioned that before. Are you quite sure that's the shape you see there?"

I am only sure that others have not always seen that shape there. On some of the maps the island does indeed—I would swear it—have the shape of the human heart. But on others it looks more like a spleen or a lung or even a kidney. I do not know how to account for this; the maps done by early explorers can perhaps be dismissed as merely errors in mea-surement, but what is one to make of the fact that even those done from aerial photographs seem to differ in shape? Per-haps it is the effect of the tides, of the contours of the island being altered from high tide to low tide, so that the shape of a map would depend on the hour of its making, though the island seems to be of sufficient size that even extreme tides would not be likely to cause such radical differences in the perceptions of its shape as these maps evidence. Not from a heart to a kidney, no. Is it necessary to conclude, then, that the shorelines themselves are flexible, as free and adrift as the island itself? Off on its own journey of exploration, a counterpart to the way it was itself explored during the early days of American colonization, the island moves at will now through the fluid shapes of the human interior.

And therefore I am wholly at a loss even to know from day to day the shape of the world I inhabit. I have no means for measuring its dimensions except for the length of my own erratic stride, which seems to become, each day I leave here to roam the island in search of acorns and mushrooms, strangely shorter and shorter, quicker and quicker. Nor do I have any way of achieving perspective on the shape of the island as a whole. And even if I did, could I be certain, as I

paused to transcribe it, that the outline of the island still con-
formed to the shape I had just seen? Neither can I speculate
with more than the broadest sense of approximation upon
where we are. *We*: the island, the forests, the beaches, the
house, the pigs, myself. We are adrift at sea, in the Atlantic I
presume. There are, of course, no navigational instruments
to be found here in the house, no more than could be found
in anyone's house, I suppose. Who would have ever thought
it would be necessary to chart the course of this place?

It is not necessary, of course. It is only necessary for me to
follow the course of the island, of which I am so thoroughly
a part. I would not have known how to use the instruments
of navigation had I found them here, anyway—where, after
all, should someone like me have gained experience in map-
ping his way across the open, unmarked seas?—but I suppose that somewhere in the library I might have found the
means to instruct myself. Many of the books, unfortunately,
have already begun to rot on the side porch in the windblown
rains that we have frequently encountered of late, and I cannot tell, for I am out in the woods so much of the day, whether
the pages have been turned by the pigs or the wind. Sometimes pages are torn away. Whole books, my own among them,
are missing. I am not sure how to account for this, but it makes
little difference; there is enough reading material here to last
a lifetime, and besides, are we not now in the very process of
developing an entire community of writers on this island?
Soon, soon, I hope, I will be able to begin reading them.

Meanwhile, I do not much bother anymore to check on the
books I leave out for them, and I have become increasingly
random in my selection process, one day a handful of books
from this room, the next day a handful from that, no cookbooks, of course, but I do not want to be anyone's censor.
Eventually everything must be read, encountered, and whether
they do so on the side porch or elsewhere is not for me to
say. Perhaps the books have only been blown around the far
side of the house by the wind or covered by leaves. For the
weather is changing. We are still moving south, I believe, and
even more rapidly than before; I am sure of it. It has begun

to grow quite chill again, though my skin seems to be toughening to accommodate to the weather, and I have not yet found it necessary to put my clothes back on. My shoes I have not seen in months, not since the day I left them by the side of the road. The constellations I can see on the rare cloudless nights are mostly unfamiliar, the constellations of the Southern Hemisphere no doubt, though I can still recognize Gemini clinging to what I take to be the northern horizon. It has become increasingly difficult for me to turn my head upward to look at the stars, however; it is naturally far more important for me to keep my eyes on the ground, where I move and feed and live. The pigs no longer seem to take any particular notice of my presence among them. Neither do they appear to be jealous of my ability to pick food out of difficult places and gather considerable quantities of it in my hands; their own rough snouts are, I am certain, far superior instruments for digging up hidden morsels from unsuspected places. I believe they have begun to eat more mushrooms. If they are offended or amused by my return to the house each evening, they have not shown it in my presence, nor do they seem at all inclined to enter the house themselves, though I leave the doors propped open at all hours now. The pantry door I keep closed, however, for I have begun to find it increasingly repulsive to pass, each day, as I exit down the hallway, those shelves of canned goods layered with dust. But I am out of the house at dawn every day now, when the chill of the night still lies in the forests and ground fog rises from the swamps and the moist earth, mingling at times with the heavier mists that sweep in off the sea. For days at a time, lately, all vision is obscured, and standing on the far edge of the lawn looking out to sea, I am often unable even to confirm that we are at sea, that there is anything at all out there in that dense and milky whiteness. Only a day or so ago as I stood there at dawn, I had a sense of something strange and enormous passing close by. The waves lapped suddenly high against the shore, and for a moment I was certain that a great ocean liner must be moving slowly by, quite unaware of our presence. Then, briefly, the fog thinned. It didn't clear but simply seemed to thin out enough so that I could see a shape far, far larger than that of any ship, a great, craggy, mountainous shape, which must have been as large as our island itself, giving off a sudden chill in its passage. It could only have been a giant iceberg, drifting northward out of the southernmost seas, but it made no difference. I trotted off to join the others in the forest, for that is where I live, and for the first time in many days caught a glimpse of our black queen in the distance, across a wide clearing, as the fog began to lift. It was as close as I have been to her since our meeting in the road at the far end of the island many months back. Doubtless, most of her time is still occupied giving lessons to the young ones. Such an important undertaking as that cannot be neglected. But even in that crowd, across that wide and still fog-shrouded clearing, I did not fail to be impressed by the sheer power of her presence. She stood tall and dark and strong, even in the distance towering above all others. Just before she turned and left the clearing and disappeared into the forest, she swung her majestic head about to look directly across at me, where I leaned forward gathering tree mushrooms off a fallen oak. She is very beautiful. One day I know that she will come closer again, that she will speak to me, in whatever way she has learned how to speak, whatever language she has mastered or chosen for the occasion. Perhaps she will merely leave me once again a single word etched in the sand. I will read it, with amazement once again, and then once again nothing, nothing, will ever be the same. The power of language is such that even a single word, taken truly to heart, can change everything.

# Game Time

The Dutchmen are playing an intrasquad game on a field laid out in a pasture outside of Murray, Kentucky, and no one is watching them. Their bus, blanketed with the dust of country roads, sits parked on the dry grass behind the chicken wire backstop, and everybody on the A Squad who isn't at bat or on base is sitting either beside it or inside it, taking advantage of what small protection it offers from the August sun. Inside, it's a toss-up: tinted windows that don't open and a management rule against running the air conditioner when the bus isn't rolling on the highway. The driver, who once thought he could never see enough of the great Marcus Teasley at the plate, is stretched out asleep across the long backseat, while outside, under a cloudless sky, Teasley, sweating heavily from a long afternoon under the summer sun, steps to the plate and lashes the first pitch on a line between the left fielder and the center fielder, neither of whom moves in pursuit of the ball. There is no point wasting any energy chasing it down: with no outfield fences, any ball that gets past the outfielders will roll for hundreds of yards on the hard-baked surface.

Finally, about the time Teasley is jogging around second, the center fielder turns and begins to walk slowly in the direction the ball has rolled. Behind him, the entire A Squad wanders toward the shadow of the bus, Teasley crossing the plate and bringing up the rear. The pitcher and catcher sit side by side on the brown grass in front of the mound, while the B Squad infielders go desultorily about their usual task of picking pebbles out of the dirt and tossing them into foul territory. Just as the other two outfielders look across at each other, shrug, and begin to turn about to trudge off and join the search, a cry arises from the distance, and, soon after, the ball itself comes sailing toward them in its long arc, bounces once, is picked up by the left fielder, examined briefly, then relayed on one more low bounce to the shortstop, who starts it quickly around an infield clearly enlivened by the fact that the ball has been found and they will not, once again, be inflicted with the fine the management has begun to levy this past month on each member of the defensive team for every lost ball.

*     *     *     *     *

Caracas, the rookie utility infielder who plays shortstop for the B Squad, climbs back aboard the bus after taking a piss in the little round comfort station at the freeway rest stop where the bus is violating a sign that orders NO OVERNIGHT PARKING. In spite of the open door and the cool breeze outside and the star-filled sky, it is dark and stuffy on the bus, and Caracas, wandering down the deep trench of the aisle, lifting newspapers off the faces of his sleeping teammates, hears their meager vocabulary of oaths mumbled many times over by the time he finally uncovers Sticks, the pitching coach. Sticks, an old man who claims he never sleeps anymore, doesn't budge. Caracas shakes him by the arm that dangles over the edge of the seat, tugs at the bill of his cap, and finally wiggles his finger around in Sticks' ear.

"Mr. Sticks," he whispers when he sees the old man has his eyes and mouth wide open, "where we are going now?"

Sticks sighs and fumbles around for his newspaper, but Caracas has let it drop to the floor of the aisle. "You woke me to ask me that?"

"Sí."

"I don't know. What difference does it make? Kentucky."

"Already we are in Kentucky," whispers Caracas, a serious student of geography.

"Well, shit. Tennessee, then."

"Only three days ago we came from Tennessee."

"Whattaya want, Caracas?" Sticks begins to raise his voice. "West Virginia suit you?"

24

## Game Time

"Mr. Sticks," says Caracas, still at a whisper, "already we have played in West Virginia everywhere that it can be played in West Virginia."

Sticks sighs loudly, slouches, droops back to a whisper. "Then we will just play where the bus takes us, Caracas. You know that as well as I do."

Caracas, like everyone else on the bus, knows that. He also knows that in six months, including spring training, of living in the United States, where he once dreamed of traveling regularly from coast to coast, he has seen only four states and no city bigger than St. Augustine. He—who probably has studied more North American geography than any of these Yankees and even now carries an atlas in his suitcase! Five states, he corrects himself, remembering their drive through Georgia. Utah, he suggests now, New Mexico, Arizona.

"Jesus," says Sticks, "in the desert? We'll all die."

Caracas, whose own first name is also Jesus, is of the opinion that they are already in a desert, already dying, that signing with the Dutchmen, a team that the sports papers he used to read accorded an almost mythic stature, was the biggest mistake of his life. In Cuba, he thinks, I am a hero for sure.

He retrieves Sticks' newspaper from the floor, spreads it carefully over the old man's face, then starts toward the front of the bus, thinking that since he can't sleep at least he can get his box of Ritz crackers out from under his seat and go sit in the cool breeze at one of the rest stop picnic tables and eat them. But just when he is almost there, Brownstein, too groggy with sleep to be much aware what he's doing, staggers back onto the bus and flops down in Caracas' seat. Caracas hesitates. He can still go for the Ritz crackers, try to slide them out from between Brownstein's feet, but if Brownstein wakes up in the process, he will probably grab them for himself, make enough noise to wake up the whole bus, and pass the box of crackers around over Caracas' head. Brownstein is six feet eight, a hulking reliever with a lifetime ERA so low it is only spoken of in whispers, and already at spring training Caracas has viewed, through the little glass window from the inside of a clothes dryer, Brownstein's idea of a practical joke.

So after a while Caracas shrugs, turns around, and heads for the back of the bus, where he knows he'll find an empty seat. When he passes Sticks, he stops for a moment, lifts the newspaper again, and hisses a single word: "Iowa." But he doesn't know whether the old man hears him or not.

*    *    *    *    *

The bus driver, cap pulled down over his eyes, executes a graceful and complex maneuver, sweeping away from the freeway on a broad, cloverleaf exit ramp, crossing the overpass, then arching down around the next entry ramp so that the bus is back on the freeway once again, headed in the opposite direction. On the east side of the bus the players begin to grumble, finding themselves bathed in sunlight just when they thought they had guaranteed themselves a morning in the shade. But when Apple, the manager, stands up in the front of the bus, neat as ever in a blue Palm Beach suit, white shirt, and striped navy and white tie, everyone shuts up. Apple's voice is as neat as his clothes, and when he speaks, he can be heard all the way to the back of the bus, even through the rumble of the motor and the hum of the air conditioner. He tells them, briefly, that they are on their way to play in Iowa for a while. No one makes a sound, not even Caracas, who is sound asleep with his head bouncing against a sun-filled window. Apple sits down in the front seat, across the aisle from the driver, then stands back up and announces tersely that first they will play a few games in Indiana en route.

From somewhere toward the rear of the bus, Blatz, the A Squad catcher, slouched down out of sight, wakes Caracas with a string of belches that sound like a great ocean liner going down in a swamp. Blatz, whom it seems no one ever gets out when the big hit is needed, is from South Bend.

*    *    *    *    *

By the time the Dutchmen reach Iowa, with a three-game Indiana stand behind them—in an abandoned high school football stadium in suburban Jefferson, a pleasant glade in

## Game Time

Brown County State Park, and an unplowed field nobody knows where—the season total stands at 102 wins for the A Squad and none for the B Squad. In order to satisfy the management and keep on getting paid, they still have sixty games to go.

Are the players discouraged? Since there is no official scorer, they spend a lot of time keeping their own statistics, except for Teasley, who hasn't picked up a pencil since spring training, and arguing about them, except for Teasley, who doesn't seem to care enough to argue. When informed on the bus ride across the fertile farmlands of southern Illinois that he is currently batting .537, he simply shrugs. His teammates on the A Squad, all of whom are hitting anything from fifty to a hundred points above their lifetime averages, constantly rail at the fates that prevent this fruitful season from ever being set down in the record books. Caracas, listening from across the aisle to the statistical agonizing of these superstars, decides that Teasley is a real gentleman for remaining silent and not reminding them who the opposition has been all summer.

As for the B Squad, the pitchers have discovered some interesting devices in the Pandora's box of mathematics that have allowed them to do wonderful things with their earned run averages. The rest of the squad consoles itself with the truth: namely, that they are lucky not to have spent the whole season riding the bench. Still, thinks Caracas, it would be nice to win *one* game before the season ends.

\*     \*     \*     \*     \*

Iowa is even hotter than Kentucky and more heavily farmed, and as they bounce along country roads looking for a suitable place to play, Sticks throws the dirtiest looks he can manage across the aisle at Caracas. Unfortunately for him, Caracas sits in a window seat and has Mulcahy, who is as big as an Iowa barn and an admirable first-base target to throw at, beside him.

Finally, in disgust, what with the air conditioner making more noise than cool air and dust blowing in through the open door, Sticks climbs down into the aisle, leans across

Mulcahy, and hisses at Caracas, "Jesus damn you, you little runt, don't never make no suggestions to me again. Nobody crosses Sticks twice."

Caracas, who has never seen so much corn in his entire life and is staring out the window in total amazement, cannot imagine what's gotten into Sticks.

Mulcahy shakes his head, rubs his eyes, and says, "Huh?"

"Listen, Mulky," says Caracas excitedly, "it is our lucky day today, I think. Today we gonna beat them for sure. Ask who is pitching."

Mulcahy reaches across the aisle and taps Sticks, who has resumed his seat, and asks politely who is pitching for their B Squad today, but Sticks, whose throat is dry with anger and clogged with dust, cannot talk. He coughs and draws an *X* in the air with his finger. *X* is Marvin X, who says he has no other name and wants to be called Killer. The rest of the players think he's lying about his last name, just another rookie trying to get attention, but they believe the killer part because he's averaging almost one hit batter per inning.

"See!" says Caracas, bouncing in his seat. "I tol' you so."

He looks out the window again at the tall, green corn, as high as the bus on both sides of the road. Caracas is convinced that if they would just stop the bus here, anywhere, they could all get out and walk down a cool, green aisle between those beautiful, even rows of corn and find just the ball field they have been looking for, with a beautiful grass infield and smooth, hard base paths and the outfield green and trimmed and a covered dugout with an ice water drinking fountain. But he knows better than to suggest this to Sticks.

\*    \*    \*    \*    \*

At 1:30 most of the players are sitting in the prickly, hard stubble along the first-base line, listening to Brownstein's portable radio, which is now broadcasting market quotations for shoats and barrows. Soon the weather report will come on and inform them that it is only 97 degrees, not the 105 that Brownstein has been telling them it is. Gimmelman, the very model of an all-star ballplayer and a gentleman, stands in the midst of another group by second base, pointing out to them where the larger rocks in the outfield are, the ones too deeply embedded to be moved. He points out the small gulley in deep center field and the barbed wire fence that angles sharply in toward the foul line in right: "Ground rule double for anything that bounces through it."

He fans himself futilely with his cap, looks across to the little camp table set up along the third-base line, where Apple, in his blue suit and tie, is pouring himself a cup of Kool Aid from the orange plastic cooler, and mumbles, "C'mon, let's get this going."

Apple has already been approached by several of the players with this same end in mind, and in each case has consulted his printed schedule and shown them where it says that today's game is supposed to begin at 2:15.

"I don't make the rules," Apple enunciates. Then he tells them that they will follow the schedule; it is their duty; it is, in fact, the very essence of baseball to follow the schedule.

"In baseball," says Apple, who tries to be something of a philosopher at times, "schedule is destiny."

"Unless it rains," various emissaries mutter, but they trudge back to report the news to the players lounging along the first-base line, knowing that not once all season have they had a game rained out, that under these dry, blue skies it will not rain today, that they are, anyway, at the mercy of an omnipotent schedule that can easily accommodate such natural phenomena as rained-out games.

"Ninety-fucking-seven," says Fridley, lying flat on his back in the stubble in mask, chest protector, and shin guards, "Jesus!"

Caracas, squatting beside him, doesn't care. He is hardly sweating, and the field sits atop a small rise from which he can see miles and miles of green cornfields stretching out in all directions. It is like being in a gigantic stadium full of quiet, respectful, green fans. He would like to see an Iowa farmer in bib overalls step behind the plate and shout "Play ball!" instead of Sticks, who has a pitcher's notion of the strike zone.

"Look at Killer," Caracas smiles at no one in particular,

pointing to where Marvin X is lying on his belly in the taller grass nearby, his face in his glove and his left hand clutching a ball behind his back. "He so warmed up, he whacked out. He won't kill nobody today. Maybe get someone out for a change, no?"

\* \* \* \* \*

In fact, the Killer's change-up works like a dream today, and for four innings he has the A Squad swinging at air. What he throws them isn't really a change-up because he isn't changing up *from* anything, but the hitters are so frazzled by the heat and so wary from Marvin's past appearances—most of them sport multiple bruises from his wild fastball—that they stand back from the plate with the sweat dripping in their eyes and can't seem to get their timing right. Fridley signals for fastballs and curves and sliders, but Marvin just keeps throwing that one slow pitch, and after a while Fridley stops hiding his signals, hoping that if they steal his signals and keep on thinking something else is coming, maybe he and the Killer can continue to get away with just playing toss for a little longer.

In the top of the fifth, with Teasley leading off, Caracas, standing with his hands on his hips at shortstop, realizes that Marvin, who is currently zero and twenty-six for the season, has not had to pitch from the stretch even once. They have all been striking out, waving their bats feebly at Marvin's gentle tosses, or bouncing weak rollers to the infield, and even if his own teammates have been doing pretty much the same, a scoreless tie this far into the game is a unique event in this long season. However, Caracas watches Marvin bounce the first three pitches slowly up to the plate and then plunk Teasley on the hip with the fourth. Teasley, his wide face a dark river of sweat, looks around, puzzled, as if unsure whether that little flick at his hip could really have been one of the Killer's pitches, then follows Sticks' pointing arm to first base.

Fridley pushes his mask up on his head and shuffles out

to the mound. "OK, Killer, time to quit this shit and start bringing it."

"Hey, man," says Marvin X, "I'm putting everything I got on it. You seen anyone hit me yet?"

Fridley looks at Marvin X, who tucks the ball in his glove and wipes his face with his cap.

"It's the heat, man," explains Marvin as he twists his cap back on his head. "Everything just *looks* like it's slow motion."

To Caracas, edging in toward double-play depth at short, it seems that it takes Fridley forever to walk back, head bowed, from the mound to home plate, another forever to adjust his mask and squat down behind the plate and begin flashing signals. Even the signals appear so slowly that Caracas has much time to roll each one over in his mind, consider its implications for him—move left, move right—and then reject it in the knowledge that Killer is just going to throw his change-up anyway.

Killer does, and Gimmelman, a right-hander, hauls his bat around so slowly it looks to Caracas as if he's swinging through water and pulls the ball down in the dirt and out toward short. Watching the ball make its way out to him, counting the seams as it bounces once, twice, three times, and knowing that it's hit too slowly for a double-play ball, Caracas tries to say "Shit" but can't seem to get the word to leave his mouth. Finally he gloves the ball, heaves it to second, watches as Kepler poises in the air, enfolds the ball in glove and hand just as he floats downward to tick the edge of the bag with his left foot and execute a perfect, graceful pivot, each movement flowing clearly and distinctly into the next as he unfurls his right arm for the throw to first. No, man, thinks Caracas, no chance, don't throw it away. But Kepler releases the ball anyway, though it doesn't seem to Caracas that he's gotten anything behind the throw at all until he looks over and sees the speedy Gimmelman, drifting airborne through one of his long strides, still a long way from first. Gimmelman descends, thrusts, strides. The ball sails gently through the air. Caracas watches. At long last it disappears into the deep folds of Mulcahy's big mitt. Sometime afterward, Gimmelman crosses the bag, and still later, Caracas, turning, sees Sticks, halfway down the line toward first, slowly beginning to raise his right fist, thumb out.

*    *    *    *    *

An inning and a half later the B Squad creeps into a one-run lead when Caracas slogs his way down to first through the thick, hip-deep molasses of afternoon heat, unable to comprehend how, at that pace, he has beat out a roller past the mound; takes second on a wild pitch and sits resting on the bag while the A Squad infield pokes around in the corn-field behind home plate for the missing ball; trudges over to third after having so much time to watch Marvin's sacrifice bunt shape up that he knows exactly to the inch where it's going to roll; and scores on Kepler's fly to straightaway cen-ter, though he has to keep shaking his head in order not to fall asleep while he's standing on the bag waiting to tag up as the ball drifts slowly down out of the sky.

Back on the bench, on the ground actually, sweating as heavily as if he's really been *running* the bases, Caracas feels like the game has been going on for many hours already. Apple, in blue, strolls behind the squatting players, and Ca-racas, without turning his head, weakly raises one finger and mutters, "We number one."

Whoever sits next to him—Caracas doesn't turn to look because he realizes that the way things are going he will have to take the field again before he manages to swing his head all the way around—picks up the mood of possible victory: "Next week the Astrodome."

"The Kingdome," calls the next voice down the line.

And after a while, just about the time Caracas figures he might have gotten faced around that way, he hears Killer's voice come drifting up the line, saying, "Yeah, man, King-dome come, that's when, kingdom come."

*    *    *    *    *

It seems to Caracas, taking the field in the top of the seventh, that the season has already lasted an eternity and that this particular game is lasting another eternity. Watching the other infielders trot slowly to their positions like the ancient burros that used to haul firewood through the streets of the village where he grew up, that still no doubt carry those same mountains of dried sticks on their backs through those same dirt streets, Caracas begins to think that perhaps there are indeed some things that last forever: that he will never see those burros again because he will never get out of the game that's going on right here and now; that if his mother sends him a postcard it will take forever to reach him because the Dutchmen will still be in the late innings of an intrasquad game in a pasture surrounded by cornfields somewhere in Iowa; that though he has always heard that nothing lasts forever, maybe baseball is different.

Caracas thinks that he will make a joke about this eternity of baseball, that he will say they are playing for the wrong team, they should be playing for the Angels, but by the time he manages to summon up Keenan's name from his mind and shape the word in his mouth and expel it into the air and watch its slow passage through the dense heat in the direction of the third baseman, and by the time Keenan raises his square face heavily in response and begins bit by bit to turn to the left, Caracas has forgotten what he was going to say.

Besides, he notices that Sticks, behind the plate, is gradually probing his way through the syllables of "Batter up!" and that Blatz is circling behind him, dragging his bat through the dust as he trudges toward the batter's box. Blatz is still wearing his shin guards, and during his tedious passage from behind the umpire out into his open stance beside the plate, Caracas considers calling out to him to remind him that he still has his shin guards on. But finally, watching Blatz slowly hoist his bat to his left shoulder as if he were tugging a tree trunk out of the ground, Caracas decides to say nothing. It will take an eternity to get the words out, an eternity for Blatz to look down and see that he is still wearing his shin guards, an eternity to step back and remove them and take his stance at the plate again and haul his bat up onto his shoulder.

What a world, thinks Caracas: it takes forever to get through an eternity.

\*     \*     \*     \*     \*

Caracas wants to spit, to get rid of some of the dust that feels like it has been in his mouth for ages, perhaps since the day he was born. He wonders how long it will take him to work up some saliva. Eternity is very dry. He will have to get his tongue in motion first, somehow. He is leaning forward, on the balls of his feet. The Killer is in the midst of his windup, where, it occurs to Caracas, he has been for some time now. A number of items creep across the foreground of Caracas' consciousness like advertising banners pulled by tiny airplanes out over the ocean along a crowded beachfront, the way he has seen them in Florida, looking like they are hardly moving against the wide expanse of sky, though he knows they have to be going at a pretty good speed just to stay up.

The first item informs him that at least he has added three more states to his itinerary, all of them beginning with *I*. On the next banner the *I* becomes the figure *1*, reminding him that they are still leading one to nothing. In an eternal game perhaps they will always be leading one to nothing, even though they are just the B Squad and he is just a rookie. If the season were just beginning today, if this were their first game, he could have a wonderful year, though he doubts this sort of schedule would qualify him for Rookie-of-the-Year honors. After a season like this, he wonders, will he still be a rookie next year? At this rate, perhaps he will be a rookie forever. He will never get a raise, play in an All-Star game, win a Gold Glove award, become eligible for a pension as a ten-year man, never make the Hall of Fame, play in an Old-Timers game, autograph baseballs for kids in Venezuela.

On the other hand, if the game lasts an eternity, the A

## Game Time

Squad will have forever to catch up and even to take the lead, to grab number 103 and leave the B Squad winless forever. It is one long season, says the slowly waving banner. Don't I know it, thinks Caracas, watching the Killer release the pitch at last. Any one of these guys, says the banner, is likely to tie it up with a single stroke. One swing, thinks Caracas, following the rotation on the Killer's change-up as it slowly spins its way toward the plate. And all the time I am thinking, he tells himself, how I have signed aboard numero uno.

Like still another little banner, Sticks' call flutters out toward shortstop: "Strike one."

Already, thinks Caracas.

  *   *   *   *   *

There is a story Caracas remembers in which the sun is held up in its passage across the heavens, nailed to one point in the sky until certain events on the earth beneath it can be enacted, but for the life of him Caracas cannot recall where he heard that story. He is looking straight up into the sun now, into whose fiery, open mouth Blatz has popped up the Killer's high, outside, one-strike pitch, a change-up naturally. Caracas, watching the ball climb steeply off the end of the bat, knew right off that it was his. He knew exactly what its trajectory would be. He knew that on this hot, windless afternoon he could take it without moving more than a couple of feet. He knew that Keenan would be circling around behind him to his right to back him up, that Parrish would be gliding in behind him from left field. He knew, could almost feel, the rest of the team relaxing around him on this sure out, and, flipping down his sunglasses as he arched his head upward, he waved both arms in a high V, signaling that it was his play.

Then the ball disappeared into the sun.

Caracas, waiting for the ball to reappear, cannot believe that story about the sun standing still belongs to the Yankees, who are always in so much of a hurry to get on to the next day that he can only imagine them pushing the sun faster and faster across the sky, greasing its tracks, attaching rockets to it. If it were up to them, he thinks, they would get rid of the sun altogether and play nothing but night games. In Caracas' limited experience, after a night game it is always the next day practically before you know it.

But neither can he recall that the story about the sun belonged to any of the Indian legends his aunts used to tell him in the village where he grew up. In those stories the sun was always, for sure, one thing that could not be messed with. But just to make certain, Caracas sifts through half a dozen of those old stories in which the sun plays an important part and which he has always enjoyed and remembered in great detail.

He is right, of course, but still the ball does not come back down out of the sun.

Perhaps, thinks Caracas, it is a story that does not belong to either the Indians or the Yankees but to the great game of baseball itself. He would like to glance around at the rest of the infielders to see if they think this is an interesting idea, but he does not dare to take his eyes off where he last saw the ball as it disappeared into the sun. He can feel that the drop of sweat that was cresting on the tip of his nose just as Blatz popped up is still there, and he thinks: naturally, I must have got the story wrong, because if the sun is not moving, how can anything beneath it move? It occurs to him that in the perfection of its poise and waiting, this is the most *baseball* moment of his life. There are moments of equal poise and grace in bullfighting, he knows, but they are gone almost before it is possible even to be aware of them, whereas baseball offers, above all else, this miracle of time in which he now stands transfixed, wherein even the most humble event, the infield pop-up, the easy out, becomes an absolutely perfect moment, into which everyone can lean together—independent of huge stadiums and glaring lights and tv cameras and roaring crowds—and know, *know*, follow, admire, share the graceful, predictable arc of events, the perfect, eternal moment, the towering pop-up rising to disappear at the peak of its climb into the open, motionless fire of the sun.

Caracas stands beneath the sun, hands high above his head, glove open, ready to snatch and trap the ball in his grip should it ever descend, but he does not believe he will ever bring his arms down again.

# The Serious World and Its Environs

Though from time to time we re-entered the serious world—the world of appointments and lectures and hotel reservations, the world of pain and money and doctors—it hardly seemed possible to do so, even with a conscious effort, in the presence of Mr. Banarjee. None of us felt too well on our arrival in Benares; all the way from the airport to the hotel our stomachs served as silent but persistent reminders that there *was* a serious world. And, in fact, nothing in it *looked* more serious than Mr. Banarjee, the mystery of whose meeting with us at the airport has never yet been satisfactorily explained. Yet there he was as we stepped down onto the hot pavement of the runway: "I am Mr. Banarjee."

All three children stood in a line, shading their eyes from the late afternoon sun as they stared up at him. Just behind them, I momentarily did the same—for he towered over me as well—before reaching over their heads to shake his hand, which went limp in my grasp.

At the Imperial Hotel, to which he escorted us in a pair of umbrella-shaded bicycle rickshaws, Mr. Banarjee followed us and the porters to the large room the children and I were to share, where he examined every bed, nightstand, closet, and cranny before pronouncing his satisfaction with an exaggerated nod of his head. Then he stood in the center of that high-ceilinged room, beside our pile of suitcases, and, apparently not knowing what more to do, managed to look more uncomfortable than I have ever seen any man look, before or since.

The children, meanwhile, had decided to lie down with their not-quite-right stomachs till suppertime, which was rapidly approaching; the heavy folds of mosquito netting hanging over their beds moved gently beneath the huge, wooden fan that circled slowly overhead as Mr. Banarjee and I withdrew to the lobby. There I sat on a rattan couch beneath yet another giant fan, only to find that Mr. Banarjee had remained standing, so far above me that I soon found myself back on my feet again in an attempt to diminish the distance between us. Looking up to him—as I had to do even standing—in the center of this empty lobby, I thanked him for his assistance and invited him to stay for supper with us. He replied that he could not. I thanked him again, expressed my regrets that he would not be joining us for the meal, and then, trying to ascertain something more about the role he had so quickly assumed in our lives, asked him if he were from the University.

"Yes," was all he answered, leaning slightly forward from the waist, his shoulders hunched up, his eyes darting about the lobby.

And was he, I then inquired, a member of the English department?

"No."

What he looked like was a wanted man, waiting for the police to pounce upon him at any moment. And I wanted something from him too: I wanted to know more than his simple *yes* and *no* had revealed. But in a foreign country you do not press too far, too fast, lest you spoil everything by crossing certain boundaries clearly demarked to everyone but yourself. You wait, allowing for differences, believing that sooner or later everything will come clear and you will know what you need to know. But it was a stiff and quiet waiting, in which I soon found myself feeling as uncomfortable as Mr. Banarjee looked. Both of us stood awkwardly in the middle of the lobby, Mr. Banarjee looking over his shoulder from time to time, though there was no one else about except a clerk and a couple of porters, until at last the children reappeared, prompt as always where their meals were concerned and considerably enlivened by their brief rest. Perhaps it was only the flight that had upset their stomachs; the two boys professed starvation, the little girl, who always waited to see what was being served before admitting whether she was hungry or not, said she felt fine, and I was ready to sit down myself.

Mr. Banarjee accompanied us to the dining room. Once more I invited him to be our guest, and once more he declined. He stood stiffly by as we were seated, hands, wrists, and white cuffs hanging far out of the sleeves of his gray suit jacket. This was the foreigners' hotel, the usual comfortable and oversized legacy of British rule, and, as had usually been the case in our travels, there was no one else in the dining room.

"Are you sure you won't join us?" I asked, thinking maybe I had missed the proper amount of urging. The children all looked up expectantly; we were alone together most of the time on this trip, and a new face at the table always provided some welcome variety, especially since most of the people we met, particularly the Indians but other travelers like ourselves as well, seemed to genuinely enjoy talking with the children, who, for their part, genuinely enjoyed the adult attention.

"No," said Mr. Banarjee, edging a few awkward steps to the side as the waiter approached with the soup. The children—no, all of us—continued to glance up at him, in silence, as we ate. Gray of face, tall and gaunt and terribly solemn, leaning always slightly, stiffly, forward from the waist with an air of deep concern, he looked, I thought, rather like an undertaker. But here in Benares, where fire and water did the job and most people undertook their own ends, it came across as the half-starved, half-comic look of an undertaker in a city that needed no undertakers. Somewhere between the fried fish and the mutton curry, he disappeared. I neither heard nor saw him go, but when I looked around after the flurry of changing courses was over, he was no longer there. The children had not been aware of his departure either.

"But," said the oldest, examining a piece of gristly mutton on his fork, "we have a name for him. We call him The Gray Ghost."

When we arose from breakfast the next morning, Mr. Banarjee was standing at the entrance to the dining room—not exactly *at* the entrance, but off to one side, in a corner of the lobby actually, looking about as if to make sure no one was taking undue notice of him. I—we—were not unaware of the nature of that look ourselves. We had come to practice it ourselves, in fact, as part of the comic routine of our travels each time we came to earth in a new city; we had found ourselves looking over our shoulders in airports in Madras and Bangalore and Bombay and Delhi and whispering out of the corners of our mouths, "Are they on to us yet?" "Did anyone see us?" Of course, they—usually the United States Information Service Cultural Affairs Officer and Someone Important from the University—were always on to us; serious and solicitous, they gathered us together with our luggage, confirmed our upcoming plane reservations, and whisked us away by taxi to hotel or university, always one of the children whispering into my ear—and each other's—always a little too loud and giggly: "Curses!" "Next time we'll give 'em the slip!" "Don't worry, we'll never tell the secret formula." Hysteria among the travelers, consternation for the hosts: "Is everything all right? Would the children like a toy?" The children giggled louder; palaces, jet planes, ruined forts, elephants, markets, servants were their toys these days. The whole world was something to be played with, and I, I was not the least bit ashamed to say (though I would not have said it in the back of the taxi with the Professor and the Cultural Affairs Officer), played with them. "Gonna give 'em Whitman today, Daddy?" "No, he did Whitman in Poona; it's Poe's turn today." "Poe, ugh!" Over their heads, as if unable to hear them, the Professor inquired solemnly about the subject of my lecture, and the USIS man hoped I wasn't being pestered with too many touchy political questions.

Mr. Banarjee—The Gray Ghost of Benares, as I too had already begun to call him in my mind, though so far we had seen much more of him than of Benares—seemed wholly unconcerned with such serious matters, making it all the more difficult for me to keep any focus on the excuse for this trip. Not a word from him about the University—or about literature—and already this morning the children were giggling around him in the lobby: they had put ten rupees apiece into a pool the night before, betting on how soon Mr. Banarjee would appear today. Cajoled into joining them, I knew I had lost when we awoke in the morning with no tall, gray shape dimly visible through the mosquito netting. Now Nicholas, the winner, was showing his little handful of change to Mr. Banarjee and excitedly explaining, as Mr. Banarjee bent down over him with an uncomprehending smile, how he had earned these riches.

If Mr. Banarjee was offended by—or even aware of—our having made a game of him, either that morning or any of the later occasions that enlivened our stay in Benares, he never showed it. He merely patted, or almost patted—I don't believe his hand made actual contact—each of the children on the head and said, "Come, I will show you Benares."

And so he showed us the holy city of Benares: holy goal of the holiest of pilgrimages, holy place for the holy end of lives both holy and unholy. On the ghats, the broad stairways leading down to the holy Ganges, many waited for that end with no intention of ever returning to the villages from which they had begun their pilgrimages. On the ghats, as we saw from the flat-bottomed scow that took us slowly up the river, some had reached that end already. Flaming pyres celebrated their holy achievement; cooling mounds of ash briefly memorialized it. The river, slow and thick and brown, looked as if it could be walked upon: not a function of holiness, I feared, warning the children time and again to keep their hands out of it. Our pilgrimage, I wanted to make clear, was not the same as everyone else's here. The innoculations we had received against the world's serious diseases had not altogether alleviated my fear of them. I kept imagining the children lifting the hands they had been trailing in the river to brush them against their mouths and, beginning to favor death by fire to death by water myself, was happier when we were ashore once again.

That this was not our end, that we were only tourists—tourists with a small job to do tomorrow or the day after—was easier to remember as Mr. Banarjee led us through the narrow, packed streets above the ghats, his tall, gray form a clear beacon in the midst of saffron robes and bright saris, the flash of colors from shops whose wares overflowed into the streets, and trays of glittering trinkets. The twisting little streets were tight and vibrant with life, the children's faces flushed not just with the heat of the late morning but with the excitement of all these people, all these things, all this activity, and I trailed a few steps behind to watch that none of them got swept away in all this brilliance and motion.

Were we, I called ahead to Mr. Banarjee, moving away from the river now?

"Yes, away," he replied, and I knew it, for the tide in these streets flowed strongly against us: toward the river from which we had just returned, the end of their many pilgrimages, toward death.

At an intersection so narrow and crowded that even those who walked their bicycles had great difficulty maneuvering through, Mr. Banarjee stopped us and bought, from a street vendor so old and shrunken that she was hardly visible above her tray of goods, a small wooden toy for each of the children: a trio of tiny birds—different-colored birds for each child—mounted on a disk that spun them around, their heads bobbing, when its handle was twisted. I tried to pay, feeling certain that he could ill afford even the single rupee, but he pronounced his usual "No."

As the children experimented with their spinning birds, I watched the opposite corner, where another vendor, a sturdy young man, was doing a thriving business in sealed brass vials.

Mr. Banarjee spoke softly from somewhere far above and behind my right shoulder. "They are filled with holy river water."

So, I thought, as we wandered slowly out of the market streets in search of a taxi to take us back to the hotel for lunch, even those who do not plan on staying take a little bit of this holy death away with them. An answer of sorts to the question that, in good taste, I had refrained from asking Mr. Banarjee: Is there life after holiness? It was a question that had often bothered me, I thought, as once again we settled ourselves into a pair of bicycle rickshaws, Matthew and I in one, Mr. Banarjee sandwiched between the two younger children in the other: What do you do when you have reached your goal? It was not a crisis I felt I was in any immediate danger of having to deal with myself. It was a crisis of the serious world, the world against which the children and I had our unspoken pact, but it was a crisis all the same. Goallessly we were finding our way around India—by means of a seminar on Dreiser in Hyderabad, a lecture on Hemingway in Jaipur—and goallessly, having enjoyed all of these travels we could, we would find our way home. But I also recalled how I had used to anguish over the old myths of completion— over their tales of failure, rather: the failure to attain the Holy Grail, Orpheus' failure to keep his eyes fixed straight ahead for just a few more steps.

"What folly!" I said aloud, only then realizing, as I spoke, that I was staring up at the white facade of the great, and empty, tourist hotel, in whose curving drive we had come to a stop.

Mr. Banarjee, lifting Ann down from the rickshaw, refused my invitation to stay for lunch. "I will go now."

While I paid the drivers, the children gathered around to thank him for their toys, and when he straightened up above them, I said to him, not questioning, "You will take tea with us this afternoon." He nodded, dipping his head jerkily forward, not unlike the toy birds the children were spinning, then he turned and walked stiffly away.

While the children napped after lunch under the heavy folds of mosquito netting and the throbbing, wooden ceiling fan, I sat on the quiet veranda, thumbing through my lecture notes on Melville, drowsing a bit myself, and thinking of their mother, that citizen par excellence of the serious world. If she, who struggled so desperately with her own goals, had accompanied us, how would she have dealt with this particular city that was, for so many, the goal of goals? For her, the chief goal was honesty, but once she had it—and she got it, not often, to be sure, but she got it—she did not know what to do with it, where to go with it, how to live with it. Well, I wondered, what *do* you do with your Holy Grail once you've found it? Set it on the mantle? Put it in the trophy case? Fill it with cut flowers? No longer an object to seek, it becomes merely an object to behold; sought after, it is motion, life, but found, it is only a dead thing. Completion is stasis: the Grail discovered, Eurydice rescued, and what do you do then, when nothing more is called for, when the story stops—accomplished, perfect, eternal, frozen, dead. Holy City, Dead City. Folly indeed, not to make that silly misstep just before the goal is reached: and sully the flesh, distrust the serious world, undermine the truth. Honesty, it occurred to me, was too easy, anyway. Any child could do it; it was, in fact, mostly children who did do it. If there had to be goals, why not at least make them, as perhaps those myths taught, acknowledgedly unattainable ones? Escape from the urban confines of the serious world, for example, even though it was clear that the best one could hope for was a pleasant life in the suburbs.

On that wide expanse of lawn opposite the veranda, in front of the hotel, where dozens of huge crows strutted, bobbing their heads and ruffling their glossy black wings, two darkskinned gardeners, barefoot but dressed in white, like barbers, trimmed the grass along the edges of the drive with small scissors. On an acre of lawn, they weren't a dozen yards from where they had been working when we left the hotel in the morning. It would be a week or more, I could see, before they would work their way down to the far end of the drive and then begin the lengthy circuit back along the street front and eventually up the other end of the circular drive toward where they had been this morning. Round and round they could go in this way forever, trimming away at the edges of this broad lawn of pale, fine grass where tomorrow morning—when I returned from lecturing on Melville and turning aside questions on American intervention in Southeast Asia— I would find the children romping wildly about, smashing croquet balls between each other's legs.

I grew to like that frivolity of grass as I sat there: to keep it not just alive, but quite perfect, in this hot, dry, dusty city of the dead, and beyond that to have it attached as a piece of decoration to an obsolete and nearly empty hotel that was itself merely a hand-me-down bit of extravagant decor from another era, was not merely an endless task but a pointless one as well. The crows, strutting stiff-leggedly about the lawn, seemed to enjoy it, though, and I was with the crows.

When I looked up, I saw Mr. Banarjee, stiff-legged as the crows and as gray all over as they were black, striding down the gravel drive. I had traveled east for almost a year to arrive at Mr. Banarjee, and in a day or two we would be turning about to head west again: New Delhi, Bombay, and, eventually, home. And he was as perfect a goal as I could have imagined: I had never known he was there, I couldn't take him away with me, I didn't seem likely to know more about him when I left than when I first met him, and I could already see that I wasn't ever likely to forget him, either. I squinted up into the sun at him as he stepped up onto the veranda in front of me, wishing he would move over just a bit so I could be in his shade—but he wasn't likely to be a particularly useful goal, either—and wished him good afternoon.

"It is teatime?" he said hesitantly, his arms poking out on either side as if he either wanted to shake hands or wanted to avoid shaking hands. I rose, spilling my lecture notes from my lap, to take his limp, bony hand in mine.

"Melville," I apologized, looking down at the papers strewn across the veranda floor.

"The children," he exclaimed, looking over my shoulder and naming them as they came into view, single file, from the lobby door: "Nicholas, Matthew, Ann." That he had confused the boys' names seemed to diminish neither his delight nor theirs on seeing him.

A hotel staff that far outnumbered us served us a sumptuous tea on a white wrought-iron table, around which we sat in gleaming, white wrought-iron chairs, in the very center of the lawn: sandwiches and cakes and iced drinks the children knew they were forbidden to drink, and, of course, the tea itself, which I poured when Mr. Banarjee declined the honor with a bob of his head and sudden look aside—at the hotel, the grass, the crows, the road, I couldn't tell. I was hardly sure, for that matter, whether he was really sitting there with us; he appeared to be perched not actually in but some fraction of an inch above his chair, as if ready to take flight at any moment and join the trio of crows perched on the veranda railing where I had been sitting or the bevy of waiters hovering discreetly in the background, on the edge of the lawn, alert for any signal from our table. It is only now, long after, when the dramatic finale to our teatime no longer sticks out as the major event of our visit to Benares, that it occurs to me that, in a setting that rigidly, in spite of the times, observed the sharp distinction between foreigner and native, white skins and dark, there was no way that Mr. Banarjee, hovering grayly between us like the ghost the children had dubbed him, could have settled comfortably into his gleaming lawn chair and allowed himself to pour the tea and summon the servants, as I did, to replenish the cucumber sandwiches, which he soon devoured.

The gardeners had removed themselves when the servants first appeared with the table and chairs, and the crows too, those that had not taken clumsy flight to the veranda railing or the hotel roof, had drawn back some twenty-five or thirty feet from where we sat, observing, like the servants, some rule of respectful distance known only to themselves. The children, accustomed as they were to deferential treatment from people wherever we traveled, were nonetheless amazed at how the crows, huge and shiny black against the pale green of the lawn, maintained their own stiff and distant formality. They wanted to toss crumbs out to see if the crows could be tempted to approach closer. I objected, pointing out that since they were paying more attention to the birds than to their manners they were already distributing a wealth of crumbs on and around the table. Mr. Banarjee responded with a slow smile, and then Ann shifted the conversation, remarking that her mother, if she had been there with us, wouldn't have enjoyed this teatime at all: "She's scared of birds."

I looked around. There were certainly a lot of them, large and black and not really very far away. I looked around: beyond those on the lawn were others on the railing, the roof, the fence that separated the hotel grounds from the street. I looked around—as I was always, it seemed, looking around, missing the Professor's intense question from the back of the taxi about the American expatriates or losing my place in my lecture notes on Whitman's "Passage to India"—and thought, as Ann had reminded me to, of her mother, as in fact I did almost every time I looked around and dropped the reins of a conversation, a lecture, an argument. If she had been here, she would have sat firm and erect in the midst of this circle of birds and kept herself properly focused on the food and the talk, as she had always wanted me, too, to keep my eyes fixed straight ahead, on the truth—for just a few more steps, always just a few more steps. But I had looked around.

When I looked back, Mr. Banarjee was folding his handkerchief and the children were applauding. He had shown them a trick, a bit of magic I would never have expected of him, sleight of hand I would never have dreamed his stiff hands capable of. I smiled: marvelous things happened when you looked around, sometimes the things you saw by looking around and sometimes the things you missed. The children, of course, wanted more, but Mr. Banarjee apologetically explained that that was the only trick he knew. For more, they too would have to look around. Even the food and tea were finished, so we rose and started to stroll back toward the hotel, the circle of crows separating to make room for our passage and the children circling Mr. Banarjee to demand more of his presence the next day.

"I will take you," he promised, "while your father is making his lecture."

Naturally I wanted to know where he was going to take them and why, as well, he wasn't going to be attending my lecture himself—after all, he had claimed to be a part of the University that was sponsoring my presence here—but before I could ask him—and needless to say, I did not remember to afterward, and if the children ever told me where they went with him while I was rendering serious judgments on the Melvillian view of the universe in a stuffy, overcrowded lecture hall, I no longer remember that, either—there was a sudden, shattering commotion behind us, and we all looked around to see the crows attacking the tea table. They swooped down upon it like great, clumsy bombers, shattering plates and cups and strewing silverware over the lawn in their search for the crumbs of cake and bread we had left behind. The servants, too late to prevent considerable damage, came rushing across the grass, flailing their arms about and swinging white napkins in the air to drive the crows away.

"That is crows," announced Mr. Banarjee when we turned away, at last, from surveying the damage they had wrought.

"That is crows, that is crows," chimed the children, as we climbed the steps to the hotel veranda. This time we looked around to find Mr. Banarjee still standing at the foot of the staircase.

"Now I am going," he said.

And that is Mr. Banarjee, whom I never saw again. The following morning he picked up the children after I had been whisked away in a taxi to my lecture—in the company of a white-haired Professor of English busy asking me about the influence of Eastern philosophy on Melville while I stared out the window at bullock carts and sari shops and had to ask him to repeat every question—and brought them back before I returned, alone this time, in yet another taxi. I always meant to write him a note of thanks for his kindnesses to the children, to us, but I neglected to get his address. Thank-you notes are part of the serious world, like anniversary cards and confirmation gifts, and though I think about my obligations in these areas from time to time, the usual fact is that when the day is past, I find I have quite forgotten. Only this year have I finally managed to get down on my calendar all the important family dates. Does that mean I have begun at last to make my peace with the serious world? (Will I remember to get those dates down on my calendar again next year?) I do not think I have ever really been at war with the serious world; I was raised in it, after all, like all the rest of us: the world of braces and insurance policies and wedding ceremonies and oil changes and college degrees. But what I was thinking when we boarded the plane from Benares to New Delhi with the conspicuously awkward shape of Mr. Banarjee nowhere in sight, though we all paused for several minutes at the top of the loading ramp looking about for one last glimpse of him until the stewardess in the shimmering blue and gold sari ordered us inside—what I thought about while trying not to worry about the condition of the ancient DC-3 we were locking ourselves into with frayed seat belts—was how I liked to believe that I was always more comfortable living as close as I could manage—and some could surely manage more—to the edges, rather than the center, of the serious world, being, to whatever extent I could manage (and the airline tickets, charged to American Express, which the stewardess was now examining, were no extent at all), in it but not of it, moving through it without evident goals or limitations ("I think my stomach's starting to hurt again," whispered Ann from the seat beside me as the motors roared and the plane taxied out toward the runway), but not fleeing or fighting it either: a Gray Ghost of the Serious World.

# The Main Chance

1.

Where X came from, it was believed that each individual had one chance, and only one chance, in life.

"Pretty slim pickin's," his new acquaintances generally said when he told them about this.

Not really bad, though, he wanted to show them, especially considering what he had learned about some of *their* beliefs, most of which seemed to revolve around a central concept of no chance at all: of having been doomed or damned, take your choice, from—or because of (take your choice again)—birth.

What he generally told his new acquaintances by way of self-defense was, "At least it's totally democratic. *Everyone* has a chance."

But what complicated the benevolent premise of his own belief system, and thereby kept him from wanting to go into a lot of detail about it with these people, was the fact that you never knew when or what your chance was. Naturally this created a lot of anxiety at home, as well as a lot of sleeplessness: you didn't want to be caught napping when the big chance finally arrived. And if you weren't absolutely one hundred percent alert, you might miss it even if you were awake. People took a lot of pills to stay awake and alert. You could tell which ones were the pill poppers from the way they walked the streets, not just the nervous bounce in their gait but the way their eyes darted left and right without rest, always on the lookout for it. They were practically everyone.

On the other hand, there was always the continuous worry that even if you were all chemed up to the peak possible height of awareness, you still wouldn't know it when it came, because you wouldn't know exactly what you were looking for, and so it could be here and gone again even before you knew what it was.

If you ever knew. That was the other constant worry. What if your chance had already come, and you didn't even know it? What if it had come when you were in the second grade, and instead of knowing it, spotting it, grabbing it, you just kept working on your arithmetic homework? What if it came when you were making love the other night, when you were too preoccupied with coming yourself to attend to what was passing by right then and therefore ended up settling for brief physical delight—terrific, no doubt, ecstasy even, but brief— and losing your one chance for . . . for what?

Everything, that was what they said. For everything.

## 2.

X thought this opportunity for an exchange residency on Earth that his government had offered him was his chance. That was what he actually told himself when the offer came, in person, by the Head of the Academy of Interplanetary Exchanges: "This is It." He did not say it aloud, which would have been considered arrogant and in poor taste, but he said it to himself, even while he was expressing his humility and gratitude to the Head; even while they were having tea and discussing the countless picky little details that travel always involves, he was saying to himself, "This is It." That was what people always said when they thought their chance had arrived: "This is It." There was even a popular video show called "This is It!" that reenacted true stories of the arrival of the big moment in cases where people saw it and knew it and said to themselves, "This is It." At least the producers claimed they were true stories.

But what X and everyone else, at least everyone else of average adult intelligence, knew was that you can't really know, can you? Oh, you could spot something arriving, something that clearly seemed to you to be *your chance*, and say to yourself, "This is It!" Only you couldn't really know, could you, until later at least, whether that had been your chance or not. Later, when you saw what the results were. And how much later was later? Next month? On your deathbed? Later still? All you knew was that you were going to get your chance, just like everyone else. You didn't know whether you would recognize it when it came or even be aware of it in retrospect. For all you knew, you would just take it in passing, unthinkingly, not even knowing it for what it was, the way you might idly spear the last bean on your plate with a tine of your fork and pop it into your mouth and swallow it without even being aware of what you were doing. And later on, when you were leading the good life, or whatever kind of life it was that taking your chance led you to, and people said, "Now there's someone whose chance came and who saw it and grabbed it and just look at the results, will you?" and when they approached you to ask you about the big moment, to learn what it was like, because, for the same reason they watched the video show so devoutly, they wanted to know what it was like for other people so they would be ready for it themselves when it came, what could you tell them? That you didn't even know—still didn't know—when or what it was, things had just gotten better and better for you, it seemed to have started about a year ago, maybe a little longer, but you couldn't remember anything specific that had happened, anything you'd really done differently, any . . . any . . . It?

No, you couldn't tell them that. That was cruel. The only thing worse than the despair in those words was an admission of your own ignorance. And even where X came from, it was not generally believed that the blessed are stupid. So you probably made something up. And what X thought was that if what you made up was good enough, sooner or later it probably ended up being reenacted on "This is It!"—which did half a dozen individual dramatizations on each weekly show and so needed a lot of material. X, who, like everyone else he knew, was an avid follower of the show all the time he was growing up, could see how they got it.

3.

Twice in his own past he thought he had got it. Twice he had said to himself, "This is It," and then had only one thing to hold onto in the time that followed: relief that he had only said "This is It" to himself. That had been one of the reasons he had been so careful not to give away any sign of his recognition when the Head came to tell him that he had been selected for the Earth exchange. Having learned his lesson twice in the past without having made a fool of himself to anyone but himself, he wasn't about to make a fool of himself before the Head.

The first occasion he could and did, later, easily rationalize to himself as merely the folly of youth. Only in the folly of youth could you believe that your chance came with melodramatic intensity, that it was heralded by flaming meteors, choirs of angels, volcanic explosions, civilizations in flames. In X's case, it was the choir of angels. Only one choir member, actually: she came rushing into the backstage dressing room at his high school ahead of the others, while the rest of the choir was still onstage taking its bows, and he didn't even know what he was doing back there when she came in, probably ducking out of the concert was all. She didn't see him, because even as she came sweeping in through the door, she was pulling her choir robe over her head and reaching for the dress she had left draped over the robe rack, but the fact that she had nothing at all on under her robe struck him with as much impact as if, in the brief moment while she tossed the robe aside and pulled her dress down over her head, a tidal wave had swept through the room without so much as upsetting a chair or leaving more than a small puddle behind. She was gone before he could blink or rub his eyes, and everything was exactly the same as before, except for the purple robe crumpled on the floor in the opposite corner, except that everything was completely different and he was saying to himself, over and over again, as he hurried out the door and down the hall toward the rear exit of the auditorium, "This is It, this is It!" He got the door open just in time to see her climbing into a car parked at the curb. She settled herself into her seat, buzzed the door closed, then looked back as the car started up. The light from the door X was still holding open fell across her face, and he saw that it was only

## The Main Chance

Y, who sat next to him in math class. The car turned as it lifted off, and X saw Y's mother at the controls. Y continued to sit next to him in math class all that year and the next, too, as well as in a variety of classes they both took later at the Institute, but that was all there was to it. It took him several years to fully accept the fact that that was not It.

The second time came when a waiter in a small restaurant where he was lunching alone spilled an iced drink in his lap. It was just the sort of trivial way in which he knew, by then, it would come, when it came. He leaped up out of his chair purely by reflex as the icy liquid soaked his thighs. On his feet, he saw at once that everyone in the restaurant had turned toward him to see what the commotion was, and on their faces he saw, well, it was not so much what he saw as *that* he saw: he saw each face in the little restaurant etched with a kind of absolute clarity, such a purity of line and contour and color that even as the waiter was attempting to brush his pants off, he was thinking to himself, "This is It, this is It for sure." Later, out on the street, walking slowly to let his pants dry in the afternoon sun, he realized that he saw every face he passed on the walkway exactly as he saw those faces in the restaurant and that, in simple fact, that was the way he had always seen them. This time it did not take him very long to understand that this was not It, either.

But when the Head came in person to his apartment to inform him that he had been selected for the residency exchange with Earth, he knew for certain, even as the Head droned on in its unpleasant nasal whine about the responsibilities of the exchange, that this was It. Absolutely.

## 4.

The only thing was, it did not seem to be working out that way so far.

Not that X hadn't made a good life for himself on Earth. In fact, he hoped his Earth counterpart in the exchange program, a famous Swedish beauty whose face once regularly graced the covers of the magazines his wife and daughters now read, was doing half so well back where he had come from. He had married—a lovely woman from Philadelphia, where he had never yet been—selected a suitable job from among the multitudes that were offered him, and thereby had his own suite and staff in the home office of a national insurance company in Milwaukee, with a salary appropriate to the upper floor on which he worked and a certain amusement in being able to make daily use of the actuarial skills he had only developed as a sort of hobby back home. He had a sprawling—*sprawling*, if he remembered correctly, was precisely the word the real estate brochure had used—house on an acre lot in suburban Shorewood; he had two brand-new cars and had long since mastered the rather simple art of maneuvering these clumsy, earth-bound vehicles; he had a variety of motorized equipment for maintenance and amusement—tractors, lawn mowers, snow blowers, snowmobiles, outboard motor boats, all sputtering their way noisily through his days on the amusing old internal combustion principle—and he also had, much to the amazement of many of the sponsors of the exchange program, three daughters, each one of them a living demonstration of, among other things, his own humanness. One of his greatest pleasures came from observing the difficulty people had deciding whether his daughters resembled him or his wife most. He wondered if the Swedish beauty had produced any offspring yet; at times, in fact, he wondered if he couldn't have been more happy just being mated to the Swedish beauty, his match-up in this exchange after all, somewhere out in space, perhaps midway between their two worlds, far from all this paraphernalia: garden implements and staff meetings and French wines. He had managed the automobile just fine, but French wines—which were all his friends, his wife's friends actually, drank—he had not yet learned to manage. Drinking French wine always gave him a headache. At home—he still thought of that as home—he had never known what a headache was.

The sprawling house and its equally sprawling grounds were also, he had learned, a headache. At least that was what all his acquaintances told him at the dinner parties he and his wife attended: keeping a house was such a headache. It was a theme that had been played at every dinner party he had attended since they had moved into the area, a theme that was replayed just as persistently as the theme of his own belief system, which everyone seemed to continue to find inestimably curious no matter how many times they heard it. He had become equally adroit at sidestepping both subjects. As far as his beliefs went, that was just the way it was, and unless you were willing to wade into the whole morass of complex personal details, which these people clearly weren't— they couldn't seem to linger on any single subject for more than three or four minutes—there was nothing more to say. And as far as the house-headache went, he hadn't found that to be so at all. He rather liked being out at the far back end of the lot on a sunny June day like this, high in the seat of the riding mower, its spluttering engine isolating him from the rest of the world as he cut a wide swath through the blue-grass out beneath the elegant specimen plantings of the trees of northern Europe.

He just wondered if this was all his chance, when it came, when he took it, was supposed to lead to.

5.

No one he knew, of course, would have ever questioned it—that much he knew himself. The beautiful, raven-haired wife! and the salary she brought in besides! The daughters full of straight teeth, good grades, and naturally curly hair! The house, cars, job, vacations in the Caribbean! The re-spect—how it flowed to him from friends, family, fellow workers! And even more than that, the honor: to be the first one to have come here, as a permanent resident, from so far away! And to have done so well! And to fit in so perfectly! To be just like everyone else! And him an alien.

That was what it was, he told himself, wasn't it? He turned the key and shut off the mower's engine and sat there in the lake of sunlight that filled the depression on the far side of the row of poplars, out of sight of the house, only dimly able to hear the hum of traffic on the freeway.

He was an alien.

He had done so well, he fit in so perfectly, he was just like everyone else, but. He was an alien.

He felt like an alien.

His main chance had come, and he had seen it come, and he had grabbed it, telling himself, "This is my chance to be something. This is It!"

But all he had managed to become was an alien.

6.

His wife's cousin Henry was a very fat man who raised harlequin Great Danes on an elegantly restored farm near Lake Geneva. He had bought the place for back taxes, built it into a showpiece over the years, and now either rarely left the place, except to show his dogs, or welcomed guests there. X knew that he himself was only there because his wife had phoned her cousin to get some help in luring X out of his depression. As had happened on each of his previous visits, however, X found that Henry's primary interest in him was in debating his belief system.

"Look at this place," Henry was saying (as Henry always said). "This didn't happen by chance. I built this place up myself; I *made* this happen."

"There is a difference," X patiently explained, once again, "between chance and *a* chance."

"I thought you told me they didn't have depression back where you came from," his wife said.

"Oh, they have depression," X said.

Mostly, he knew, they had anxiety, but they also had depression. The depression came most frequently to the most extreme sufferers of anxiety, who would suddenly and unpredictably be stricken with the almost certain knowledge that they had just missed their chance. They would plunge from the peaks of long-term anxiety, from rushing about week after week with an eye on every little thing that happened to see if that was their chance, into the sudden depths of depression at the notion that perhaps the phone had rung while they weren't home to answer it (though there were many who would have argued that that didn't really constitute your chance, since it didn't occur in your presence), that they had said "yes" when they should have said "no" or vice versa, that they had erred by buying the fresh vegetable rather than the canned or frozen variety, that in some brief moment they couldn't even remember they had said or not said, done or not done, precisely the wrong thing in the face of *Its* arrival. For months they could be trapped in the very depths of depression, until gradually it began to dawn on them that they might possibly be mistaken, that even while they lay there cringing in misery beneath their blankets or deep in the soft folds of their pills, It might be approaching them, that they could no longer afford the idle luxury of lying about like this when by the very act of doing so they might be missing their chance, that they had better spring up at once, in fact, lest they miss It at that very moment. And up they would spring, as X had seen them, into the deliriums of their old anxieties again.

Show me a place without anxiety or depression, X thought, while sipping a gin and tonic from a tall glass with a picture of a black-and-white Great Dane on it, and I am on my way at once. That, indeed, would be It.

7.

Henry was showing off his multiple champion, Boozer's Main Chance IV, a routine that had to be tolerated each time X and his wife visited but that, every time, made X extremely uncomfortable. Where he came from, there wasn't a single beast, wild or tame, that stood over hip high. This monster, on the other hand, seemed to be staring X right in the eye. X only tolerated it on this particular visit, which was by no means one of his better days, because he was interested in what Henry was saying.

"It's a drag," Henry was saying. "You get to where you thought you wanted to get to and then what?"

A drag, X thought. He was glad his wife had gone off horseback riding, because she rather seemed to like the life they led. She particularly liked those enormous beasts, the dogs and horses.

Henry made the Great Dane stretch out its rear legs and lift its head. "I mean, I built this place up all by myself, out of nothing. Nothing. You should have seen it. Now look at it."

X looked. Its head was just about level with his own.

"I've won more goddamned doggie championships than I can count. I don't know what to do with all those silly trophies. They're all over this place. Basement, bedroom, bathroom. Big deal."

The giant dog had one black ear cocked sideways and seemed to be trying to roll his eyes toward his rear, where his master was standing, instead of keeping them focused straight ahead, as X knew he should.

"Listen, X," Henry continued, "do you know what the suicide rate is among the rich and successful?"

X didn't know, but he knew. Oh my, he thought, oh my, oh my, oh my. What he thought was, It's ever so much worse that I thought. What he said to Henry was, "You mean we are all aliens?"

Tears welled up in Henry's eyes. X reached forward to console his cousin-in-law, to take his fellow alien in his arms. Boozer's Main Chance IV, without so much as lifting a paw, turned his great head to one side and bit X, rather gently, in the upper arm.

8.

The wound festered. Perhaps X had encountered the one earthly item he couldn't adapt to: dog bite. The doctors were baffled. Henry was baffled: all his dogs together had never bitten a single person before. Guilt or bafflement or something else brought him to X's house every weekend as a visitor; perhaps, X wondered, Henry was wondering what would have happened to him if *he* had been bitten by that dog.

X's wife was baffled, too, though less by the incident itself or its medical repercussions than by X's attitude. Dogs bit, she knew. Horses kicked, cars crashed, children threw temper tantrums; that was the nature of the world. And sometimes wounds festered; well, medical science didn't know everything yet, and sooner or later the doctors would come up with something, even if it had to be something as radical as an amputation. But the real problem for her was that X just didn't seem to care much one way or the other.

He didn't. He lay in bed the first couple of weeks, then sat in an armchair in the living room—one or another of his living rooms—in the weeks that followed, watching the transformations of the wound on his upper arm as if it all, arm and wound alike, belonged to someone else. At first it had puffed up, scarlet and enormous; then it settled back down, black and purple, while its contours enlarged; then, gradually, it began to ooze, green one day, gray or pink the next; the edges of the torn flesh curled back, revealing weepy undersides, and for days a moist, tropical heat seemed to steam almost visibly through them; then the swelling began again. The doctors lanced it, salved it, stitched and bandaged it, and X, on their instructions, alternately soaked it, iced it, baked it under the heat lamp, kept it open to the air, or changed bandages hourly, all to the same effect. X remained curious but indifferent. The doctors considered calling in the interplanetary exchange authorities; they did not want the responsibility of what they referred to as "further unforeseen developments" on their hands. His wife was adamantly opposed, however; she was firmly convinced that it was only X's unhealthy attitude that was delaying the healing process.

X himself didn't care much one way or the other, though he did hope the Swedish beauty, off there on his home planet, hadn't encountered any strange viruses against which her body's immune system would have no defenses.

X felt as if he, too, no longer had any defenses. His medical and disability insurance, naturally enough, took care of all his needs. Not only did he not have to go to work, but there was enough money left over to hire a part-time gardener-handyman to do the maintenance work around the rambling house and ride the lawn mower over the acre of rambling grounds. It didn't make a lot of difference anyway, X thought; the pleasure element of riding lawn mowers was highly overrated. The children had come home from summer camp in

Maine only to be cleaned up, dressed up, turned right back around, and packed off to boarding school in New Hampshire. Somehow that didn't seem to X, as he observed their brief passage from his armchair in the front living room, to be a particularly sensible way of doing things, but what the heck. And if his wife seemed to be having to spend an awful lot more time at her office these days, that was all right with X, too; at least she had had the foresight to hire an efficient housekeeper who wasn't squeamish about helping him change his dressings or apply his ointments. If it had bothered her, X knew, then in all likelihood the dressings wouldn't be changed or the ointments applied.

It didn't make a lot of difference to him.

9.

The only thing that did seem to make a difference to X, as both the fall and the wound festered on, was a visit from Henry, who by now was coming most Wednesday evenings, too, and often spending the night on weekends.

"No dog show this Sunday?" X was asking him after breakfast.

"Let the handler do it," said Henry. "She gone again?"

It had been obvious to Henry that X's wife, who had in the past done so much to foster his friendship with her husband, didn't ever seem to be around much anymore. X was hardly surprised when Henry's suspicions finally crept into their morning conversation.

"Do you think she might be having an affair or something?"

X shrugged. He poured them each another cup of coffee.

"Cream, Henry?"

Henry shrugged.

10.

There was, in fact, considerable furor attendant upon X's death, less from the people back where X came from who felt that in no way could any objections ever be raised in the case of an individual who had had his chance and taken it, than from various agencies and authorities on Earth. They blamed the doctors. The doctors, when they finished blaming each other, united to blame X's wife. X's wife, packing for Greece, blamed Henry.

"He actively encouraged my husband's indifference," she was quoted as saying in the wire service articles. "If it hadn't been for him, X would have stood up for himself and done something about his problem. He was a remarkable man for taking advantage of the right opportunity when it came his way. This is a terrible tragedy. Never trust a dog fancier." The article was accompanied by a photograph of her, slender and dressed in black, entering a chauffeur-driven limousine.

"Suicide?" Henry echoed when the tv talk show host questioned him. Henry had lost a lot of weight, and the talk show staff had done much last minute rushing about in order to find a suit that would make Henry look more presentable than the one he had worn to the studio. All they had been able to come up with was the lighting technician's shiny black gabardine, which made Henry, with his pale white hands and the flesh drooping around his eyes and jaws, look like a caricature of a mortician. The host was furious. He didn't want death on his show. Nothing would kill a live tv show faster than death. This show was his big opportunity in the business, and no two-bit cadaver was going to ruin it for him. On the other hand, he needed *someone* for the next ten minutes, and Henry's barely warm body was all they had. The host, who had worked as a stand-up comic until his big chance in tv came along, knew that absolutely anything could have its funny side and figured that was his only chance now.

"So," he said, holding up his hands to display an imaginary newspaper, "you want the headlines should read: DOG BITE SECRET WEAPON AGAINST ALIEN INVASION?"

"Whatever," shrugged Henry.

Uh oh, thought the host, it ain't gonna be easy to get a rise outa this one. He mugged it up like a tv private eye, stepping out from behind his desk, with shoulders hunched, hands in pocket: "So my theory, Commissioner, is that when he saw he had no chance of saving himself from falling into the hands of the enemy, who had unspeakable techniques for extracting secret information from him, he simply threw himself on the handiest means of death, and when even that seemed to have failed, finally just gave it up, chucked it, quit the race, snuffed his own candle. You know, suicided. By willpower. They have their own secret weapons, you know."

"You know," said Henry, finally raising his eyes to where the host paced in front of him, "you may have something there."

## 11.

Because he thought this was probably his one chance, Henry, whose house or dogs had always spoken for him and who had therefore never made a public speech in his life, took it. He leaned forward, hands on knees, and stared into the tv camera and said:

"All right, I confess, I killed him."

There was a tremendous furor in the studio. In the audience, people screamed, and of the three federal agents who had been assigned to check on Henry's relationship to the deceased alien, one ran for the phone while the other two leaped up on the stage to prevent Henry's escape. Technicians peered out from behind their equipment. The director waved madly from the booth, signaling for the show to be cut off the air, but the host stepped in front of Henry and said to the camera, "Remember, you heard it first on this show!" When he paused, not knowing what else to say after that, Henry slid his chair forward and nudged him aside.

"If I may continue," Henry said, looking at the host. The host looked up at the director. The director looked over at the two federal agents huddling on the side of the stage. The federal agents looked back at the host. The host shrugged.

"Well, then," said Henry. He sat up straight, crossed one knee over the other, folded his arms on his chest.

"Well, then," Henry repeated, "to continue. I would not have you think that I am prone to violence. No. Though you would not know it to look at me now, I was once, quite re-

# The Main Chance

cently in fact, what people used to think of as the fat and jolly type. I was, I thought, a happy man. Then one day this X showed up on the arm of my cousin, his wife, that international celebrity—I'm sure you all know her. He was a dull sort of fellow, when you got right down to it, but I kind of liked him anyway. I was fat and jolly, remember. And he had at least this one interesting theory he'd brought along with him from wherever it was he came from. I can't remember, I never did have much of a head for geography. Anyway, this notion about everyone, I mean *every*one, having one big chance in life. It comes along sooner or later, you take it—bam!— you've got it made. It sounded nice, but I didn't believe it for a minute. You know, here we believe you make your own breaks, right? *I* made my own breaks, didn't I, and look at me. I don't mean now, I mean back then. This is a free country; everyone can make their own breaks, right? When is it ever a handout, like this X was saying, unless you're born rich, which some say is the worst curse of all. And of course your chance, X is telling me, may not make you rich; maybe yours will make you happy, find the right person for you, put you in the right place, bless your life with peace and tranquility, what's the difference, it's all good stuff, right? Only here is X being dragged to my house all of a sudden like a millionaire allergic to his millions. 'Hey,' I tell him, 'c'mon, cheer up. You got your chance, I made mine, what's the diff? Look at us both!' I mean, his wife was a knockout; I'm sure you've seen her on tv. Anyway, I could see he was miserable; all he wanted to talk about was his riding lawn mower. He liked it, you know, but what was it, after all? It made me realize that all I talked about was my dogs, my farm, you know. I was terrific, I was happy, I did all this stuff myself after all. But what did I do? What was all this stuff? Dogs? Houses? That was a life? When you got right down to it, I wasn't happy at all, I was miserable. I was every bit as miserable as the miserable son of a bitch who brought me this miserable news. Sorry. I mean, here he was telling me that even the absolute right chance didn't guarantee you anything, didn't even guarantee you that it *was* the right chance or that you should have taken it. I could've killed him for that.

"And dogs are very sensitive animals, you know, even if they're not a life for a grown man. Here I was, showing off my dog and X showing off his misery and me thinking, Wow, why is he telling this to me, doesn't he know what he's doing to me, and do you think my dog doesn't sense this? Maybe for him it's his one big chance to get out of this boring show-dog routine, you know, and really make his mark. So he seizes his chance, just like any of us is supposed to, right? He sinks his teeth right into it, in fact, not even knowing that he is just a projection of my own will, that he is a lethal weapon in the hands of a mad killer, just another miserable son of a bitch gobbling up his big chance and choking on it. Like X. Like me. Had to put him away, you know, so the doctors could try to figure out what he'd done to X. They never did figure it out, of course. He did what he thought was right, that's what he did. Just like X. Just like me. And where did it get any of us? Look at me, I'm wasting away myself, I used to be a fat man. I mean real fat. Hey."

By this time Henry was standing, holding his coat open, to show how little of him there was left, but there was hardly anyone left to see. The audience had begun to trickle away once they realized what they were listening to was no real murderer's confession, after all, only a lot of ranting and raving of no particular interest to them. The three federal agents were already in the bar across the street, discussing other kooks they'd had to waste their time on in past cases. Having switched the programming over to a National Geographic film on the wonderful world of whales, the director, the technicians, and all the rest of the staff were lounging about drinking coffee and getting slowly started on their clean-up chores. The talk show host was in his dressing room considering his options: pills, razor blade, gun, bridge. Henry was still on stage, addressing a dead camera and an empty studio.

"So there you have it, folks," he said, perfectly aware that there were no folks either watching or listening. "Just remember you heard it here first. This was your big chance. But you go around looking for your big chance, making your own big chance, you got to know it may just spit in your eye when you find it. That's a pisser. I don't blame any of you for not hanging around to hear this. You've got to know when to walk away, I suppose. I hope someone'll take good care of my dogs."

A whole bank of overhead lights suddenly went dark, but Henry still stood stage center, his hands in someone else's pockets.

"Maybe before I go," he said, "I should tell you about the Swedish beauty."

# Dear Ones

i.

"Dear ones," he wrote,

"I am in no mood for writing a note, but I am writing this note all the same, because I think it is extremely important for you to know that what I am about to do—what I will have done by the time you read this—has nothing to do with you, any of you. Therefore, it is not necessary for you to brood on this action of mine, or to emulate it, or to ask the endless whys. I will tell you the simple why, though I think you know it well enough already. The simple why is that once I had that which made my life worth living, and now I do not have it any longer. Nor can I have back what I once had. Nor is it necessary, I am sure, for me to go into more detail. This is not an act of sudden depression, as you may know from the time that has passed; it is not an irrational act, as you can tell from the tone of this note; nor should it be taken as a general commentary on the world, since it seems clear that at other times I have found the world well worth living in. So may each of you, I hope, in many ways. Give yourselves time, lots of time. A decision like this you only get to make once—at least if you are reasonably efficient, and I am nothing if not efficient—so it is important to take a great deal of time to consider it carefully, to explore the reasons for and the routes to this conclusion as fully as possible. Having done all that, I now choose to do this, only wanting to impress upon you, before I do so, that it is an individual choice, that it has nothing to do with any of you, that it is of, for, by, and about myself, and myself only. And that in my going I wish to leave you, as others have always left me in their going,

"With love"

## Dear Ones

He did not sign the note when he got to that point, because, he thought, to each of the people to whom he was
addressing it he was something different—father, son, lover,
friend—and there was no single term, not even his name,
that could cover all that. And when he raised his head from
staring at the sheet of paper in his typewriter and, looking
out his study window, saw the girl in the blue ski jacket across
the street struggling to shovel her car out of the snowbank in
which the plows had lodged it, he did not think, I do not
have to do that anymore, either. For he had already decided,
the last time it snowed, that he was not going to do that anymore. He had seen and shoveled enough snow already this
winter, more than he could remember from any previous
winter, and he had decided that he simply wasn't going to
shovel any more of it, no matter how much more it snowed.
Let it pile up. Let the neighbors complain about his unshov-
eled sidewalk, let the police ticket and finally tow his car if
he chose to leave it parked in front of the house on plowing
days. Just let it all happen, what difference did it make anyway? Like her death, there was nothing he could do about it
except a holding action, and very little of that, because there
was nothing, finally, that could stop what was happening.
All he could do was make things more comfortable, for a little
while, make things seem a little better than they really were,
while daily the snow clouds gathered overhead, and he shoveled and shoveled and shoveled his walk in vain.

He sat and watched, though, until two young men, joggers
in identical, red warm-up suits, who had come running down
the plowed center of the street, stopped and pushed her free.
What he was watching, he told himself, was all that movement of color: their red suits and her blue ski jacket and green
car against the whiteness of fresh snow. Then he got up and
switched off the typewriter, simply leaving the note in it, and
went downstairs and got his own ski jacket and hat and gloves
out of the closet and put them on, because whatever he was
doing, he did not like to be cold, and went out back to the
garage. He was glad it was a detached garage, and in fact
would have chosen some other method had it not been a de-

tached garage, because he knew of a case in which everyone in the house had been involved because a basement-level garage had been used, when that was not the intention at all, to involve all those other people. He was very quick once he was in the garage. Efficient, as he liked to think of himself. He closed the door tightly behind him, and got in the car, whose gas tank he had filled on his way home last night, and started the engine, and then got out and took the length of hose he had hung over a nail in the garage wall and stuck one end into the exhaust pipe and brought the other end around with him and opened the window on the driver's side a little and pulled the hose through and then rolled the window snugly against the hose to hold it in place and picked up the brick he had left on the garage floor and leaned in and rested it on the accelerator, though the engine was still racing at warm-up speed. Then he closed that door and went around and climbed in on the passenger's side and closed that door firmly, too. For a moment he thought about locking the doors, but then he realized that he could not be more firmly in the car than he already was and that locked doors would only make unnecessary problems for others. He rarely sat in the passenger seat in his own car. I am just along for the ride now, he thought. He thought he might have brought something along to read, but the light was poor in the garage and already the air was getting thick in the car. There was nothing to read but the owner's manual, which he always kept in the glove compartment. I could have looked in there, he thought, and seen how to set the idle up; maybe that would have been better than using a brick. Just out of curiosity, he reached for the glove compartment.

ii.

She kept looking behind her as she drove, first glancing in the rearview mirror, then twisting around in her seat to get a fuller look at the street behind her. Almost always these days she had the feeling that someone was following her, someone was watching her. She had that feeling just a short while ago, felt it with great certainty, when she was trying to get her car out of the snowbank, and she had stopped in her struggle to dig the snow out from under the rear wheels to look around, but hadn't seen anyone at all, until suddenly the two runners in red warm-up suits descended on her with their offers of help. She didn't really want help—she wanted to get the car freed by herself—but this was winter, and when it snowed like this people always helped each other, she knew. That was the only way you survived. Still, they looked like clowns, those two runners in red, first jogging down the middle of the street in their too-bright identical outfits, then bouncing up and down on the bumpers to dislodge her car from the heavy snow the plow had forced into the wheel wells. And they still looked like clowns when she drove off and saw them, in her rearview mirror, waving wildly at her as she pulled away. But they were not really after her, she knew, looking in her rearview mirror again just before she swung down the freeway entrance ramp. It was not necessary to think that someone was always watching her, always coming after her, but that was what she had thought constantly since the time she woke up in the middle of the night last summer and saw the face staring in her bedroom window. Even then, even while she screamed and watched him slip the window up and come climbing quickly through, gun in hand, she was thinking, now I'll never be able to look out there again, I'll always have to keep the shades drawn, I'll always think there's someone out there watching me. And ever since, she kept thinking that. She was lucky and she knew it; she had talked the intruder out of his intentions, though not out of keeping her terrified all night long and finally hitting her, hard, twice, across the face with his gun before he left at dawn. Ever since, she kept the shade drawn and the curtains pulled, but she also woke up many times in the night, every night, and went to the window and pulled the curtains aside and lifted the shade to look out and see if anyone was watching her. So far she had never seen anyone out there watching her. She had never found any evidence that anyone was following her when she walked the downtown streets, though she stopped many times each block to look in store windows at the reflections of passersby moving along the sidewalk behind her. And she had never actually found another car following her. Each time she felt certain she was being followed, had felt or seen the same car behind her for blocks or miles, all she had ever had to do was change lanes or slow down or speed up or turn off at the next street or wait a few more blocks until the car behind her turned off in a different direction. And then she never saw that car again. Still, she could not drive the length of a city block without looking into her rearview mirror, sometimes more than once, and twisting her head around as well, for a fuller view. She did not want to be victimized by any blind spots, even though she knew this was not reasonable. Just because someone was looking in my window once, she told herself, is no reason to think somebody is watching me, coming after me, all the time. Still, she thought, it is not an unreasonable fear; if someone was watching me once, someone could be watching me any time. So she watched back, always checking behind her everywhere she went. She looked back three times in the process of entering the freeway: once on her way down the entrance ramp, a second time just as she was about to enter the freeway, then again as she accelerated quickly and smoothly into the flow of freeway traffic. She turned about less than a mile later to glance at the cars behind her changing lanes to move over for the next exit and then quickly after that to check the entering traffic. She looked back twice when she reached the river, once at the beginning of the bridge and once at the end of the bridge, though there were no entrance or exit ramps on either side. All she saw was the usual freeway traffic, changing lanes in its usual erratic pattern, moving a little slower than usual, because in spite of the plows, there were still patches of snow on the roadway. She looked back in her mirror at each exit ramp; again, and over her shoulder as well, at each entrance ramp; at every overpass and underpass. When she glanced up into the mirror just before the railroad overpass, she saw the same car that had been there when she had looked back moments before. It was large and black and coming on very fast now, so she turned her head about for a better look at it. It was an airport limousine, and as she watched it, it swung out from behind her and passed her, still accelerating, in the inside lane. She turned her head back just in time to see the abutment of the railroad bridge.

iii.

Dear god, she was thinking, I wish we could walk back from the airport; I do not want another ride like that again, ever. She sat in the contoured plastic armchair in the Eastern Airlines waiting area, her fists clenched in her lap, her plaid wool coat still buttoned up to her throat. She had been the only passenger on the limo, and the driver, late and angry because he had been held up at the hotel waiting for other passengers who never came, cursed and drove like a madman all the way, running yellow lights, honking at cars in front of him, passing illegally, certainly driving much too fast for the slippery streets. Finally, when they were on the freeway, she closed her eyes, though that didn't help much either. The sounds that came to her were terrifying, though she tried to convince herself that they were just the normal sounds of high-speed freeway traffic, and the sway of the speeding limo from side to side kept her slightly off balance during the entire ride. She felt as if they were driving on ice the whole time, and once, when she heard sirens and felt the limo slow down, she hoped the police had at last spotted her driver and were about to pull him over, but when she opened her eyes, she saw that they were just slowing for the exit to the airport, the driver swearing at the clogged ramp ahead, and the sound of the siren fading quickly away behind them.

When the doctor's plane comes, she decided, we will take a taxi back instead of the limo, and we will tell him to take the side streets; we will tell the driver that the doctor has a heart condition and cannot stand fast driving. She wished she knew the city better, so she could tell the driver exactly which way to go and not have to rely on his goodwill. But she only knew the freeway from the airport into the city and some of the downtown streets between her hotel and the hospital where her husband lay, waiting for the consulting specialist to come and make the decision about keeping him on the life-support machines. Actually, she knew, however much she thought of him as waiting there, he was not really waiting, he was just lying there, in the care of various machines and people, and she was the one who was waiting. She waited, always conscious that that was what she was doing, waiting. And she trusted, too: trusted that she had done the right thing by bringing him to this hospital, trusted that he was getting the right care, trusted that the right decisions were being made for him, that the doctors were telling her the truth when they talked about his condition and their meager alternatives, trusted that some anonymous taxi driver would go along with her irrational instructions, that nothing would happen to her just now. And she was also terribly conscious that she was doing all this trusting; trusted the trusting, too, without at all knowing if that was the right thing to do.

Perhaps I'm going to die here myself, she thought, sitting in the airport passenger lounge and suddenly feeling very hot. But because she had not thought very much about herself lately, now she told herself, no, it's just the waiting that's doing that to you, throwing things back on yourself like that, that has nothing to do with anything. Except she knew that it did, that it had to do with all the long years of waiting that had come before the short time they had been together, waiting for him, not even knowing him but waiting for someone like him. No, she often told herself, waiting for him, exactly him, because finally he did come, or rather they came to each other, and then she knew what the waiting was all about, and it didn't make any difference how long they had both had to wait, not even knowing. Only now she felt like she did not know again, felt that she was just waiting, and that waiting was like your breath, like holding your breath, and you held your breath and trusted, trusted that something would happen, the right thing, and you dreaded at the same time to let your breath out, because there was always the fear that you might not be able to breathe in again, might never be able to take another breath. It reminded her of what he had said to her in the ambulance they had rented for the long, long ride to the hospital, just before they got to the city, when he was still having periods of consciousness. "I wonder," he whispered to her, "what it would be like to live with someone you love for a decade, for two decades." And she did not answer him. She was sitting beside him, holding his hand very tight, but she did not say anything, because she was suddenly afraid that if she did it would be like her breath, if she let anything out she would let everything out, if she said a single word in response to that the tears would never stop. After a little while she told him a different truth, about how much she loved him, and he smiled up at her, and she took her coat off, because after many hours of riding it suddenly came to her that they kept it very hot in the back of the ambulance, and put her head down on the pillow beside him.

Now, when she opened her heavy wool coat in the airport lounge and could feel the heat of her body escaping, it felt almost like her breath, like letting out the breath of waiting, and she shuddered slightly, and even cursed herself, saying, what a stupid way to take care of yourself, now you're going to get a chill. She had heard a lot of talk around the hospital waiting rooms and the nurses stations about pneumonia. Shit! she said to herself, not even aware that she had muttered the word aloud, but just then everybody around her stood up, because the plane had arrived and the passengers were beginning to come up the unloading ramp. So she got up, too, and walked to the metal railing beside the ramp, buttoning her coat back up as she stood there, because a cold draft came through the passageway, and waited there for the doctor, who was the last passenger off the plane, trailing up the ramp many yards behind the others, looking much older than she expected but wearing the green Tyrolean she had been told he always wore and carrying his black bag. She was the only one still standing at the railing, and he stopped when he drew even with her and leaned against the railing.

"I am sorry to be so slow," he said, breathing heavily, "I haf a slight heart condition."

iv.

The runner moved at an easy pace along the street that followed the crest of the river bluffs, a scenic drive with expensive, older homes lining one side and, across from them, an open, unobstructed view over the river valley to a similar road that traced the edge of the bluffs on the other side. Because the traffic was a little heavier here, he stayed close to the curb and kept a careful watch for oncoming cars as well as for dangerous spots on the road. The fresh snow was lovely, and soft underfoot, the way he liked it, but he also knew that it covered up ruts and potholes and patches of ice, and he feared a bad fall or twisted ankle that might force him to lay off his running for many weeks. You could run just fine in the worst of weather, he knew—in fact, he had been doing just that for years—but you had to take extra care: you had to know what the snow was like and what it could do; you had to realize that fools didn't shovel their walks and snow-plow operators and even ordinary drivers were a careless, thoughtless lot; you had to slow down a little and take shorter strides and watch your step. Always, of course, you had to watch your step. Therefore the runner rarely raised his head, and then only slightly to study the oncoming traffic, to acknowledge another runner with a brief nod, or to glance at the scenery he was running easily by. Here, below him, to his left, the river ran straight for a short way between the snow-covered bluffs and shores, and the runner, looking down on it for a moment, saw the river as a dark slash across the white throat of winter.

He wore a red warm-up suit, bright red, and white Adidas with red stripes, and a matching set of wool mittens, scarf, and ski hat, also in red-and-white stripes, all recent Christmas presents. When he first put this outfit on, on Christmas Day, he felt suddenly awkward and embarrassed, it was such an extreme change from the gray sweatsuit he had been wearing all these years, and he complained good-humoredly

# Dear Ones

that he felt more like a candy cane than a runner and that now no one would take him seriously as a runner either. But his friends, who had gone in together to buy all these new running clothes for him and Tommy, teased him back, pointed out that his face was well on the way to matching his outfit, and told him to hit the road or they would hang him from the Christmas tree. So off he went. There was fresh snow on Christmas Day, too, several inches of it, light and powdery and easy to run through, and the runner liked that and the fact that the plows hadn't been out yet, and it always helped to have Tommy running with him, too.

Somehow it seemed to the runner that two of them identically dressed would attract less attention than a single runner in such a bright, absurd outfit. As soon as he spoke this thought aloud, however, he was sorry he had said it, because Tommy just grunted and then dropped back a few paces. The runner realized at once that it had been a cruel thing to say, that Tommy hated above all to be reminded in any way of identity, and he wondered why he had found it necessary to exercise that cruel little power over Tommy just now. He could not excuse himself on the grounds of thoughtlessness, even, for he had been fully aware of Tommy's responses earlier, when side by side they had opened gifts of identical sweaters and ties and, of course, the running outfits, and even hand-painted coffee mugs with their names on them, which at least differed to the extent that one read "Tommy" and the other "Thomas."

Tommy had just grown quieter and quieter with each gift they opened, and in the end, when their friends were opening the gifts the two of them had bought together, did not even acknowledge their thanks with a nod but just sat silently, almost motionless, through the whole process until the two of them went upstairs to put on their new running outfits. And the runner felt that he would have reacted the very same way himself, if he had been the one, and he admired the way Tommy had handled it, respected his restraint, just as he respected the way Tommy dropped back a few paces, as if to declare his independence, and then kept perfect pace with him, matching him stride for stride all the rest of the way out and back. That sudden upsurge of feeling for Tommy, after his faux pas, made the runner a little uncomfortable; it was too much like self-admiration, a kind of indulgence that was just the opposite of the restraint he felt was most important. Still, he enjoyed that run, the fresh snow and the sun that broke through at the end and their steady, matched rhythms of stride and breathing, and by the time they got back, he had decided that the bright red outfits were all right after all, that, especially against the snow, they made it easier for the traffic to see them, and he told his friends about this, and how pleased he was with their gift.

Now, however, he hardly noticed the outfit anymore, and when he did, it was only to remark to himself how quickly you could get used to almost anything. He would not have said that to Tommy, but then, Tommy was a very different case in that way, and the runner did not think that even he, Thomas, could get used to being a Tommy. Running alone now, for the first time in many months, he tried to think a little of what it must be like to be a Tommy, to have to get used to the fact that you were someone else, to know that you were not just *like* someone else but were the same as that someone else, identical, cell for cell. Of course you did not really have to get used to that fact, because if you were a Tommy that is the way you always were, the way you were created. Of course, thought the runner as he moved out toward the center of the street to avoid a dangerous-looking patch of ice and slush around a sewer opening, that did not mean you had to like it. Then he edged back toward the curb and concentrated on his running and did not think much about Tommy, except for the vague sense that Tommy was not with him now. They had stopped, only a block or so after they had started their run today, to help push a little green car out of the snow where the plows had wedged it in, and then another block or so later Tommy had begun to complain that his back hurt, that he must have twisted it when they were pushing the car, and he had abruptly turned about and headed back home. That had been an odd little scene back there, the runner thought. The woman in the car had acted as if she didn't really want their help, though it seemed clear she couldn't get out of there on her own, and Tommy had held back at first too, as if to let her stay where she was, but then suddenly they had all pitched in and freed the car almost at once. Oh well, he thought, people have to do things their own way.

And then he ran on, at his steady, easy pace, along the road that followed the river bluff, not even fully aware, as he focused on his running, that Tommy was not with him, because the way they matched their pace and their breathing, even when Tommy was there, it was as if they were a single runner, he in front and Tommy hanging a few paces behind, as he had done ever since Christmas Day, but united by motion and energy and direction, just like the unity of rhythm that he felt swept him along so easily now, around the curve at the edge of the bluff and along a straight and level stretch and then into another curve, toward a bridge that spanned a small ravine, and then, seeing how hard and dry the bridge looked, totally cleared of snow, down alongside it instead, following the sliding track the children had made into the ravine and picking up a little speed toward the bottom for the dash up the opposite side, so at one with his running . . . he did not know that Tommy had come up behind him, matching him stride for stride and breath for breath, did not see Tommy's arm circle around him with its sudden flash of silver, or know, at first, why the bright red of his warm-up jacket, when he looked down to watch where he was putting his feet on the snowy track, was growing suddenly brighter.

v.

The idea of doing that whole run for just one lousy passenger made him furious, not that he would ever identify himself with those ecology freaks he saw on television or even that he was responsible for the costs of the fuel and maintenance and taxes and insurance and even the depreciation of the vehicle—he was just paid by the hour to drive it—but still, the waste was maddening. Everything was waste, finally, when you got right down to it. But the thing that made him angriest right now, because it was what he saw the most of, was the waste of all those cars racing back and forth along the freeway between downtown and the airport with only one passenger per vehicle, tons of metal and gallons of gas that could just as easily transport four or five people, or even a dozen in the limousine, moving only one person at a time instead. That was the height of stupidity. That was such an incredible waste he couldn't believe it. He didn't want to play the social conscience of the country, he had never in his life cared about politics and corruption and international affairs, and as far as he was concerned, a man's morals were his own business. And a woman's, too. He wasn't going to get into that stuff, either. But the waste, the waste was just infuriating. And driving one lousy passenger. That was such a waste, a waste of his time, a waste of his life, it made him so angry that as soon as he dropped her off at the Eastern gate, instead of circling around to pick up a load of passengers back into town at the arrival area, he just tromped down on the accelerator and headed back out onto the expressway, toward the city. What's the goddamn difference, he told himself, it's all a waste anyway. I waste my time sitting in front of the hotel waiting for passengers who never show up, I waste my time trying to talk to a passenger who closes her eyes and pretends I don't even exist, I'm just a goddamn driver, just a machine, not even a person to her, I'm just a waste of a human being. And he thought of the years he had wasted in the Army, too, waiting to be sent to Nam, where he was sure he was going to be killed; that was all any of them were waiting for in his unit, to be killed. They felt it was that certain. Only they never even left the country. The Army wasted its time training him and wasted its money shipping him around to Fort This and Fort That, and he wasted his time sitting around waiting for something that never happened, just like he wasted his time on his job now, which was not going to take him anywhere, except back and forth between downtown and the airport, which was only another kind of wasteful waiting for nothing, just like his other job, for he was a cook in the evenings, from five on, when he turned the limo over to the night driver, till closing, which usually meant two or so by the time you got the clean-up work done, and what was it, after all, hardly anything besides hamburgers anyway, and the only point of all that, of both those jobs, was to earn enough money to make sure his mother was properly taken care of, and maybe that was a waste too, for all he knew. How much of the time did she even know she was being well cared for, at home, in her own bedroom, with practical nurses around the clock?

He shouldn't be doing this, he knew, as he pulled up in front of the house. This was going to be the end of the job for sure, but the day had been a total waste so far anyway, except the hours, the money, and jobs like this were always easy to find; they never cared who you were, they knew you were just putting in your time, just like in the Army, and they never much cared, just so long as you did it fairly well, which meant not making a big deal of anything. Going home like this in the middle of the day, and taking the limo besides, was making a big deal of something, so he knew it would be the end of the job, but after all, he told himself, how long would there be something to come home to at any hour of the day, at the rate she was wasting away. He could feel the big limo settle heavily into the snow piled up at the curb as he pulled in there, and felt pretty certain that he was never going to be able to drive it back out of there, that it was stuck good, in the heavy snow the plows had shoved up against the curb and with ice underneath it besides. Well, he thought, let them come and tow the fucker out of there, then, this isn't my job anymore anyway. And he slammed the door, leaving the keys in the ignition, and went up the rough, snow-packed walk, which he had never taken the time to shovel all winter, to the house, because that was where he really wanted to be anyway. Anything else was a waste of his time.

Much to his surprise, she was lucid when he came into her bedroom, more lucid and bright-eyed than he had seen her in weeks, and even talking to him as he entered, barely a whisper, but when was the last time she had even tried to speak? Clearly, she had heard him letting himself in the front door and moving about in the living room, hanging up his coat, which was a waste because he was only going to have to go out again, but he wanted the house to look right as long as she was there, afterward it wouldn't make any difference, and she seemed to have a sense of time, too, now, because as he sat down on the edge of the bed beside her, she asked him, in her very frail voice, what he was doing home so early in the day. He looked up at the day nurse, who had been standing in the living room when he came in and had obviously seen him parking the limo, and said that the limo had broken down and the dispatcher had had to give him a ride home, and when the nurse's black face, looking down on both of them, stayed blank, he thought, good, don't waste any energy, any emotion, on that, don't waste the truth unless it does some good, and he asked her, quietly, his hands resting gently over the slight ridge one arm made beneath the covers, whether his mother had eaten today.

He knew she hadn't of course, even before the nurse shook her head. He knew she hadn't eaten, hadn't had more than a small amount of liquids for days, it must be weeks now. He knew that if it had been the night nurse he asked, she would have reminded him that it didn't make any difference any longer whether his mother ate or not, which was what she said every time he asked, which was a waste, a waste to say the same thing over and over when it was already known. It was a waste for him to ask, too, he supposed, just as anything she ate, if she had eaten, would have been a waste also, because she was that old and that hopeless that nothing was going to do her any good. Yet he kept bringing food into the house for her, kept telling the nurses what to prepare for her and how to prepare it. But it was all a waste. His being here was a waste, for she had slipped off again into wherever it was senility and weakness took her, which was only into waiting for the end, he told himself, which was a pure waste, all of them hanging around waiting for the end, his mother and the nurses and himself, when the end was just going to come anyway, and there was nothing you could do about it;

you didn't get old without knowing that, that the end was coming and that after some point what you were doing was waiting for it, which was a total waste because when it came, it wouldn't prove anything except that you had wasted your life waiting for it, that your life was a waste, that everything was a waste, a waste, a waste, that nothing you could do finally made any difference, not rage, not tears, nothing. Nothing. But he got up off the bed very slowly, very careful in his movements not to rock the mattress or tug at the covers, not to make any disturbance. And he was standing in the center of the room, waiting for the feeling to come back into his leg, which had gone numb and asleep while he perched on the edge of the bed, when he noticed that the nurse was still standing there in the doorway, with her hands clasped in front of her, and that tears were running down her face, that her face was shining with tears.

vi.

Well, she thought, sitting down on the staircase just inside the front door to take off her shoes even before she took off her hat and coat, though everyone at work is always complaining that one day is just like another, the fact is that some days, like this one, are worse than others, and on days like this you can just be glad you worked the first shift and can get away from it early. Her shoes, which she left tipped up against the riser of the first step while she got up to put her coat and hat and gloves away in the front closet, resembled a miniature snowdrift, as if the wind had blown in the front door when she entered and swept a tiny pile of snow up against the staircase, fresh snow, with hardly a blemish. That was the way she always managed to keep her shoes, and her friends at work always commented on it, how amazing it was that her shoes stayed almost perfectly white while everyone else's got scuffed and dirty at once. But what surprised her was how quickly everyone else seemed to get their shoes filthy; she couldn't see how they did it, when it seemed to her so natural and easy to keep them clean, for them to stay clean almost by themselves even. Now she leaned up against the banister and lifted her left foot and held it, massaged it in her hands, and then did the same with her right foot, though it wasn't her feet that hurt but her head. She thought she felt the beginnings of a sinus headache, though maybe it was the tiredness and strain, so she just stood there for a moment, trying to figure out which it was and listening to the silence of the house and wondering at that. It was the first silence she had heard all day long.

She picked up her shoes in one hand, sticking a finger inside each shoe to lift it, but instead of starting up the stairs, as she had intended, to see what this silence was all about, she walked down the hall and into the kitchen. She set the shoes down on the counter, then opened the cabinet above the sink and took down a glass and two bottles of pills. She took one pill from each, one sinus tablet and one aspirin, and filled the glass from the tap and swallowed both pills and the full glass of water. She put the two bottles away and closed the cabinet and turned her glass upside down on the counter, and then, when she picked up her shoes again with one hand, one finger in each, she saw that they had left dirty puddles on the counter, from the soles that had been wet with snow, so she stopped and got a paper towel and wiped off the counter and threw the towel in the wastebasket. Then she came back down the hall and started up the stairs.

On her way up the stairs she realized that her feet did hurt a little after all, that she had been on the go since early this morning and that not once had the busyness stopped, that this day was not just like all other days, that she had even been paged in the cafeteria. Now her insteps ached, and she was glad she had the day off tomorrow, before changing shifts. A day and a half, actually, since with the change in shifts she wouldn't be due in till afternoon of the following day. There were times you needed that extra little distance from it, she told herself, just that additional half day even, no matter how much you liked your job, no matter how good you were at it. And she was good at it, and she knew it. She was at her best, in fact, when things were most difficult, when several critical situations developed at the same time and the whole floor vibrated with sudden activity and it seemed like she was needed everywhere at once. She could handle that, and the side-effects of crisis—the agony of the patients, the fear in the eyes of their relatives, the growing tension in the voices of the doctors—only made her concentrate more clearly and effectively on the job at hand. It pleased her to know that the medical staff felt she was the best person to have around in any crisis and that the other nurses on her floor were not jealous of her but admired her and liked to work with her, but she was careful not to make too much of this, also, for she never felt that she really did anything to deserve it. It was just a quirk of personality, she thought, just the way she happened to be, and she could no more help it than other people, she supposed, could help getting their shoes dirty the moment they put them on.

Still, she thought, pausing at the top of the steps to feel the ache in her insteps, there were some days that were just too much for anyone. She looked in through the open door of the first room off the hall at the top of the stairs, the study, and saw that it was empty. Looking across the room and out the window, she saw that it had begun to snow again, lightly. Wouldn't you know it, she said to herself, some days it never stops. That was what had done her in today, she knew. Not crisis, really, not the many needs at the same time that brought out her greatest strengths, but the fact that it never seemed to stop. Even when sudden crisis erupted all over the place, all at the same time, you knew that in a little while it would be under control and you could pull back and collect yourself again. But today had never permitted her that final sense of relief, not till now anyway, in the silence of her own house. Today had thrust one hard thing after another at her, hour after hour, and it was not the difficulty that had finally worn her down, because she was used to working with that, used to being her best when things were most difficult, but the fact that things had come at her so relentlessly all day long, that they had piled up and piled up, one after another, not so much with a sense of being hard, though they were hard, all of them, as with the feeling that they were endless, endless and agonizing and even hopeless, and not once all day had they pulled back, had they paused in their ceaseless coming at her, to permit her those necessary moments of relief, of pulling back herself. That was what weighed on her so. That, she thought, standing in the study doorway, dangling her two white shoes from her fingers, was what made her feet ache. Then, about to step back out into the hallway, she saw that a sheet of paper had been left in the typewriter on the study desk, and, gripping her shoes a little tighter, quickly crossed the room to look down at it.

"Dear ones," she read.

# The Ascent of Man

Every time we meet like this you look at me like I'm a little bit crazier than before, but one of these times you're going to have to stop and listen to me, because what I have to say is a matter of life and death. Not mine: yours. But don't think it isn't hard on me, too. Friday afternoons I see you come out of class, Professor, that genuine cowhide briefcase in your hand and that dedicated humanist's smile on your face, you've just fielded a couple of questions even Aristotle would've found too hot to handle, and then you spot me, standing over here in my usual spot against the railing at the foot of the stairs outside Philosophers Hall, and such a look comes . . . I don't want to describe it. But how do you think it makes me feel? Suddenly you're poking around in all your pockets with your free hand like you've forgotten your wallet, and then you turn around and go rushing back into the building. Or you look off across campus and latch on to one of your colleagues who only wants to get home as soon as he can, probably the same sorry bore you've been drinking coffee with all day, and go bouncing off after him without a glance to either side. A miracle you don't break your leg falling down the steps. But you can't go on like this forever, Professor. Sooner or later.

I'd wait for you Mondays and Wednesdays, too, if I could, but I can't be everywhere at once. You're not my only responsibility, Professor. Even these Friday afternoons can't go on forever, for one thing it's too depressing, so you'd better listen. Everything I have to say is for your own good. Don't laugh.

Naturally I know it's not me you've stopped for today. I know the only reason you're hanging around here in the rain

87

thinking, why did I have to get stuck with this madman, why, today of all days, is because you're waiting for your pretty little wife to pull up at the curb, honking the horn and shaking all that puffed-out blond hair as she leans over to open the door for you, and maybe a couple of those little blond girls in the back seat, too, Daddy! Daddy! So meanwhile as long as you're stuck here you may as well listen, right? It'll help you to understand the tragedy when it comes, believe me, and even if it doesn't, it'll help pass the time, and maybe you'll forget about the fact that it's raining and you don't have a hat or an umbrella. Neither do I. It can't be helped: it was a beautiful day when we both set out this morning, but who controls the weather?

Not that you'll thank me for enlightening you about the coming tragedy, either, but I'm not your mommy or daddy, I never asked for gratitude. I just do what I have to do, and I don't even have their joy in it. Such a perfect child you must have been, too, your teachers all in love with your little curly head, your teeth so straight you never even had to go to the orthodontist, next thing they knew a Ph.D., an endowed chair at a classy institution of higher learning, a houseful of original lithographs, and a gorgeous family, absolutely gorgeous, I'm not putting you on, am I? They'll be here any minute now, right? We'll see for ourselves. Tsk, tsk.

And I forgot how your colleagues admire you, and your own children would rather read than watch television, and even now you're still the one who always gets picked first when they choose up sides for a softball game at the picnic. And humble, let's not forget humble: always you worry over your students and put yourself out for your friends, always you try to be a better person. So, you're probably asking yourself right now, so where's the tragedy? What can this crazy old son of a bitch possibly know? Didn't I just have my annual physical check-up? Haven't I been a cautious investor of my small inheritance? Nothing but Triple-A bonds, naturally. And didn't I just have the oil changed in the Mercedes, ahead of schedule even? I'm sorry.

Truly sorry: being the bearer of bad tidings is no snap either.

## The Ascent of Man

Remember what used to happen to the messengers of kings? If you detect a certain note of gaiety in my voice, a certain je ne sais quoi that seems inappropriate to our brief exchange here, try to remember that we all have to do what we can to make our lot bearable, and be patient with me. You'll learn.

As to this tragedy, now, first of all don't expect too much. Don't get your heart set on earthquakes or tidal waves or nuclear wars or invasions from Mars. For the apocalypse, who needs messengers? Nothing I have to say to you will make the 6:00 news. But don't despair. Size isn't everything. A tiny splinter. But you know this, Professor: to whom am I speaking, after all, but a Professor of Humanities? A tiny splinter, so small you could forget about it as soon as you've finished saying Ouch!, so small you can't even find it when you roll down your sock and looked for where it stabbed you in the ankle, so small you think maybe there's not even anything there or if there is it'll soon come out on its own: a tiny splinter like that can enter your flesh and slip into your bloodstream and given enough time pass through your body and tear your heart to shreds. And is it any the less a tragedy because it doesn't go Boom!, because buildings don't come crashing into the streets, because a whole civilization doesn't fall down dead beside you?

So now you're interested, maybe? Now you want to know what I'm peddling. Now you're satisfied I'm not doing the Jeremiah bit, you're beginning to wonder just what sort of petit bourgeois disaster I'm trying to insinuate into your Friday afternoon just when it's coming up on the cocktail hour. Can't I read what's written on your face? Can't I see it telling me: So go ahead, it's no big deal then, I'm stuck here for a few minutes so let's hear what this nut has to say.

Point two, he has to say, Professor, that even if it's no big deal, even if you don't expect too much, a tragedy is still a tragedy. Enjoy while you can the fact that all that water on your face is only rain. And meanwhile, should you ever feel like you need something to wipe it off with, any time, just ask, I've always got an extra hankie. But then I suppose you do, too, a nice, clean, white, freshly ironed one, even if you never use it for anything except wiping a speck of lint off your reading glasses, the better to see with.

Well, if you really want to see, want to hear, turn to me, Professor. I am the voice and the vision of tragedy, and here I am, right beside you; it's no use turning your back on me like that. Remember the splinter, Professor? The splinter also is, even if it doesn't have a three-bedroom rambler with a walk-out basement and a book that *The New York Review of Books* assures me will radically alter my perception of contemporary life. For your next book, Professor, maybe you would like to do some research on the splinter's perception of contemporary life. But maybe we should let that pass for now. We haven't got forever, and you'll be needing some time, anyway, to consider ideas for your grant proposal.

So here's an idea for you to begin with, Professor, the only idea I really have for you anyway, the one I've been hanging around a long time already waiting to present you with, small as it is, probably you couldn't be bothered to squeeze it into the syllabus of your course on Western Civilization, a mere splinter of an idea, you'll laugh, well, it can't be helped, here goes.

No one is watching.

So you're not laughing, maybe because I whispered it a little too softly because I didn't want to jab you too hard because I didn't want you doing anything sudden, understand? I'll say it again a little louder, but not too loud, understand, because this is just between you and me, I'm not trying to create a panic, just listen: No one is watching.

Well, if you're still not laughing, Mister Professor Blankface, at least you're not crying yet either, but what does it mean? Didn't they ever teach you how to react to tragedy, or is it just that you don't know the real thing when it's standing right in front of you? Ah well, I'm sorry, once again I'm sorry. It's getting late in the afternoon, and maybe your blood sugar's a little low. Sometimes I get a little dull myself this time of day. Or maybe your mind is somewhere else, maybe you're not paying attention yet. Don't worry, you will. Meanwhile . . . ah, dummkopf! Of course, what could I have been thinking of! Naturally it's hard to attend to the general when the specific is staring you right in the face, although you'll do yourself a favor, believe me, by making a connection between the two.

Meanwhile, I can see it's not my presence that's got you worried but your family's absence, and don't give me that Who? Me? Worried? shrug either; blank looks like that I've seen a million times, easy, pasted up there as carefully as twenty-dollar-a-roll wallpaper when there isn't a glue in the world strong enough to keep it from peeling. Nothing sticks to terror but terror. And maybe a little green mold when it's damp, the kind you know you scrape off but it keeps coming back right away. So stop worrying about how late is late enough to look worried and let it come, no one's watching, give it a few more minutes and then maybe you'll see your fawn-colored Mercedes creeping around the corner down there by the Physical Education Building all in one piece. Traffic's always a little heavier on Fridays, especially at rush hour, but how long can it take to get here from the shopping center? She's a good driver. It isn't really true that *no* one is watching; just a splinter of it's true, a splinter of a splinter, because naturally *she's* watching: the traffic, the street, the lights, the stop signs, the pedestrians, the little girls in the rearview mirror, adorable. But who's watching the drunk in the parking lot trying to fit his house key into the ignition of his Buick? You know that bar by the College Avenue exit? Maybe he'll never find that right key, maybe yes, usually they do. And who watched the mechanic who was supposed to be adjusting the brakes when you had the Mercedes in the shop last week? Who's watching that oil slick in front of the stop sign at the bottom of the freeway ramp? You know how it gets when it hasn't rained for a long time?

Now don't look at me like that, Professor, I don't know any more than you do, only what I've already told you: no one is watching. You think I've got a police radio concealed about my person somewhere? Where would I hide it, under this rag of a sports coat I've had all my life? Look at it, it'll take your mind off your worries. I'll bet you could never guess what these colors used to be like when I was your age. No, younger. When I ran down the streets shouting out my message, people mistook me for a shooting star, but who listens to such brilliance anymore? I could take criticism. I can keep up with the times. One-to-one relationships, that's where it's at, right? Look at us standing here together in the rain, face to face, even if you are a whole head taller. Finally you're listening to me. I could kiss you for that.

Listen, I didn't mean to scare you like that about your gorgeous family; I'm sure they'll be here any minute now. There's a million things could hold them up. Relax. No one's watching. You could go back in the building and wait in your office out of the rain for when they get here. I'll call you. Meanwhile you could be much more comfortable—you've got a little couch there, a rug on the floor that used to be in the den till your wife redecorated, maybe even your student assistant is still around, that little redhead from your 10:00 class who was in there with you this morning. I didn't know they still wore their skirts so short like that. Don't get me wrong, I don't mean to imply a thing, Professor, though who knows, if it was so, you follow what I mean, I'm not suggesting anything, just *if*, after all no one is watching, doors have locks, windows shades, it could lead anywhere, right, *if*? Listen, I'm sure you never touched her yet, but even if you did, no one was watching. Probably it wouldn't lead to anything anyway. Just remember, no one is ever watching.

And the truth is, Professor, since you insist on standing out here in the rain with me, no hat, such a pair of dummies, like we could never catch a cold and die of pneumonia, the truth is that when no one is watching, anything can happen. Airplanes go crunch just like that into the sides of mountains. Oh, was there already a train standing in the station? Gently, gently, my friend, so gently even *they* don't notice, the tide sweeps the children out to sea. And not only that, but the tin can gets dumped in the incinerator, because someone wasn't watching, and has to be retrieved finally by some poor bastard who cuts his hand on the lid and gets blood poisoning, or the inspector rubs her eyes while the assembly line keeps rumbling by and the foreman's in the john and quality control is yakking away about a new product already, or the school crossing guards stand gossiping in the middle of the street—you know those school crossing guards, Professor? They're this big, like one of your own, what could *she* watch?—so who watches, Professor, who watches? Name me a bird that looks down before it poops, or for that matter one that looks back afterward. The world is flying away from us; every time it flaps its wings whole continents shudder—go ahead, that's a cold rain for this time of year, I understand, brrr—and who's watching?

Right, Professor, now you're catching on. Naturally you don't have to take any of this personally. It's the world we're talking about. I mean, when I mentioned the coming tragedy a while back, I didn't have anything particular in mind. How could I know they'd be this late picking you up? There's a million possible reasons, and who can look out for them all? Did your wife's lover's watch stop when neither of them was paying attention to the time? Of course, that's not likely, is it, I mean that she has a lover? Or did she suddenly notice, getting dressed, the lump that's been growing unobserved in her breast? Did your oldest daughter run out of the school playground after a ball that rolled into the street? Of course, they would have called you at once. What was in their lunch at school? How many cars are blocking the fire lane at the shopping center? Maybe it's just a flat tire, not even a blowout necessarily; after all, they're only on the expressway for a couple of miles. Probably none of those things. How should I know? I'm sure they'll show up any minute now. Still, it's best to be prepared, don't you agree? Even traffic lights get stuck all the time, don't they? No one watches all those tiny little switches. I wouldn't leave just yet, Professor, isn't that your car just coming around the corner? No, wrong color, sorry, but they're bound to be here soon. Isn't the rain beginning to let up a bit? I always like the way the colors begin to change this time of day, don't you? Very soft, very gentle. Where are you off to now? Listen, I'm sure there's an explanation, pay no attention to what I said. Is it your fault? Who could possibly watch everything? There are a million possibilities; we've only begun to scratch the surface. So stick around. What good could you do anyway? We've got terrific hospitals here. Just wait. No one expects anything more of you. So you could watch one person, one place, but what about the other people, the rest of the places, the rest of the time, who's watching them? Who even watches you, Professor? See what I mean by scratch the surface? So don't turn your back and walk away from me like that, Professor, like I wasn't even here. Wait, I tell you, wait, there's more.

# The State of the Art

Frankly, I do not think I am the person to be telling you this. There were others, closer to more of the events, more familiar with most of the participants, probably more experienced than I in matters like this, capable of maintaining an appropriate objective distance. Perhaps even now they are transcribing their own versions of what happened. There is no reason to think that their versions will in any way resemble my version. But we will have to learn to live with that, I suppose. It is what they call nowadays "the state of the art."

Such a state! Such an art!

Nevertheless, since you have asked, since you have come a great distance and clearly put yourself to a lot of trouble to hear my own version, I shall give it to you as best I can. First, however, I would like to ask not to be held responsible for any discrepancies between what I am about to tell you and what others have told you or are at this very moment preparing to tell you. It is difficult enough, even in the best of circumstances, which these most assuredly were not, to be responsible for how one sees things oneself; it is quite impossible to take on that responsibility for others. I do not speak for others then. There is nothing I know that is harder than speaking for others; indeed, I hardly know how to speak for myself.

If only I knew how to begin.

Thank you, but I see no need for going back so far as that. What could be gained by implicating my parents and the unfortunate citizens of the small town in which I was reared? As for the facts, that sort of stuff is all in the records and readily accessible, public knowledge if I am not mistaken. But to what end could we drag it into a mess already so sorely entangled as this? Of course, of course, doubtless there were "causal influences." What are parents for, what is a past for, if not to provide you with causal influences? But even if we could trace each and every act, for every single one of us involved in this misfortune, back to those causal influences— surely a dubious possibility, if not an endless one—the best we would then have would be an understanding of why we did things as we did.

Whereas it seems to me that as usual we have our hands quite full simply with the questions of *What*?

Therefore, I think I will not begin at the beginning, with all its implications of causal connection to each succeeding event, which is what I can see you are already trying to ferret out, but rather with the end. We will start at the end and go backward, and you will perhaps then be able to see each event isolated from its predecessors and thus to understand that nothing necessarily follows from anything else. We could have done anything. This is what we did, however.

A dismal proposition? Let us see.

The end of the journey, as was obvious to all who greeted us at the landing—and you certainly do not need my version for this; you have the newspapers, the television, the memory of an entire nation—was certainly a dismal proposition. Harrison had to be carried from the ship on a stretcher. Ring was so disoriented she walked in circles and could not speak or respond to being spoken to. Hebb, on the other hand, babbled incessantly, though no one could understand a word she was saying. These are the people whose versions you are comparing with mine! Mitchie, I am told, did not awaken for three days. Gander made an attempt on the lives of the Honor Guard. Simoncini's body, which we had forgotten was being towed behind us, had apparently burned up on re-entry. I myself had to be pried loose from the controls. I have seen the videotapes of myself stepping off the ship smiling, standing at the microphones smiling and waving and saying something apparently intelligible. I do not understand what I could possibly have been smiling about. I do not understand how I could possibly have done any of those things. I am sure that my mind at the time was as empty as the vast and terrifying spaces between the stars.

Or between the members of the crew; between anyone, anything.

At times on our return journey we held reasonable conversations. For example, we discussed the matter of Simoncini's body, trailing along behind us at the end of a titanium cable. "Trolling," Mitchie kept saying. He appeared to be convinced we had been on a deep-sea fishing expedition and were trolling, as we returned, for whatever we might pick up. But with such bait? And in such an empty sea! God save me from ever having to make another long journey with a fisherman. His only response to our many attempts to bring him to reason was, finally, to fall asleep. That still left us with the problem of Simoncini's body, which we could not possibly keep aboard with us. The freezer was already filled with the bodies of Collins and Erickson. Simoncini had pleaded at the last not to have his body set adrift in all that pink, intangible emptiness. It was not pink, of course, though we did not stoop to arguing with him. It was certainly intangible. It was certainly empty. He wept. He knew what was out there. Even dead, he did not want to face it again. With him bobbing along like that in our wake, we were at least free to consider the alternatives. Once Mitchie nodded off, we carried on a very reasonable discussion of the matter. At one point, someone even made mention of what would happen to the body out there upon re-entry. I cannot recall all the details of our lengthy conversation. "Poor Simoncini, out there at the end of his tether," said Ring, just before she ceased to speak altogether. We were all at the end of our tether. It appears that, finally, we must have just forgotten about poor Simoncini. But he ended in a blaze of glory, did he not?

Too bad there was no one to see it.

Without Simoncini, I am not at all sure we would ever have made it back. Simoncini sick and Simoncini dead gave us all something to focus on besides our private frustrations, our private angers. From the moment he first fell ill, he became a rallying point. He was the largest and strongest and most active among us, but immediately he became our baby. We cuddled him and cooed at him, and in his presence we even began, for the first time, to speak to each other with a certain civility. Harrison refused to leave his side, but even that failed to provoke us any longer, even when he insisted on being the only one allowed to feed him. Not a word did I hear spoken against Harrison's selfishness. Not a snide remark against the perverse obsession he still maintained with feeding us. Our hearts broke, in fact, to see how Harrison himself, so totally involved with caring for the man who had once been his dearest friend, no longer seemed able to eat, how his once corpulent body seemed to be wasting away even faster than Simoncini's sturdy frame.

I am sure he has managed to put it all back on by now.

Even while we were loading the ship for the voyage home, I knew that Simoncini was a dead man. I could see it in the way Hellerman was responding to him. Simoncini was standing in the loading bay, and Hellerman was handing up to him the bodies of Collins and Erickson. Everyone else was already on board, preparing the ship for departure. When Simoncini came back to the open bay after placing the two bodies in the freezer, he reached down to give Hellerman a hand up into the ship. "You next," he said. I was standing just behind him, waiting to make sure the hatch was properly closed and sealed. Hellerman looked at the hand Simoncini was extending to him as if it were covered with shit. I could see Hellerman's predicament. He was always a very polite man, and though he did not want to take Simoncini's hand, he did not know how to refuse it. He did not want to hurt Simoncini's feelings, but clearly, considering who Simoncini had just pulled up into the ship, he did not want to be "next." Finally, he looked over Simoncini's shoulder and spoke to me instead. "I did not sign on a death ship," he said. Simoncini still stood there, leaning slightly forward through the open hatch, his hand still poking out into that sullen, pink-tinged atmosphere. "Individually, yes, I suppose so," Hellerman continued, "but as a group activity, no thank you." Then he turned and walked away. A ship's length away, he wandered into a puddle of pink haze. It flowed up and over him until he could no longer be seen. "Schwartzie!" I wanted to call out after him—we always called him Schwartzie—but I knew it was no use. I nudged Simoncini out of the way and pulled the cargo hatch shut. I stood there until I had heard all its airtight seals snap into place; then I left the cargo bay as quickly as I could.

I could not stand to linger any longer in the midst of the smell of shit.

It was obvious to all of us that it was time to be going. Months and months and months on the journey out, and many more months yet on the journey back. It seemed so foolish, Mitchie insisted, such a long way to come for what amounted to little more than an overnight stay. He was right, of course, no matter how selfish his motives. There was a little stream he wanted to fish. He was sure it was perfect for trout, or whatever passed for trout on this planet. He was forever talking up the glories of pan-fried rainbow trout. Our culinary choices, I reminded him, were already a primary source of our dilemma. "Well all right," he whined, "whatever I catch, I'll throw it back in." "No!" I shouted. He sulked. It was the beginning of the end for Mitchie, though perhaps even now he is stalking some icy Rocky Mountain stream in his hip-waders. Some people never learn. For the moment, I thought I had an incipient mutiny on my hands, especially when I noticed that Gander had picked up Mitchie's fly-casting rod and was flicking it back and forth. Later, she confided that she had only been thinking of hooking Mitchie himself with it. I am not at all certain of the efficacy of that particular approach to the learning situation. Meanwhile, it was not I that quelled the possibility of rebellion, but terror. The pink fog was beginning to wander in and around us again where we had gathered near our ship. Not fog, actually, but discrete little clouds, more or less the size of large pillows, though at times they drifted together and spread out at their edges and so came more to resemble fog. There was no way to fend it off. It simply drifted over you, immune to the wildest waving of your arms, flowing between your fingers, across your face and through your hair. The most terrifying thing about it was that though it looked thick and heavy, looked like it should have felt like cotton candy in its stickiness, it felt like absolutely nothing, nothing at all. If you closed your eyes, you would not even know anything was there. But you did not dare to close your eyes, for fear that when you opened them you would see nothing but pink, dense intangible pink, all about you.

Fear, though much maligned from what I hear, can in fact be very useful, especially as a shorthand reminder of what has happened before and therefore can happen again.

As soon as I returned to the ship, it was clear what had happened in my absence. Three concentric rings awaited me, with not a surprise in any of them. From time to time, I have had some surprises, but here, I thought, were only the inevitables. The inner ring was composed of the bodies of Collins, Erickson, and Desnick, laid out in a little circle, or triangle if you will, head to foot. The middle ring, surrounding them, was made up of monsters, no more than a dozen or so of them. The outer ring was my crew, or what remained of it. Only the middle ring was demonstrating any sign of concern. Their great heads hung down, and clouds of the pink fog rolled down their foreheads and over their creased faces and across their shoulder bones, making it look as if they were crying rivers of pink, cotton-candy tears. The bodies in the center looked quite serene, as if nothing had happened. Those in the outer ring were doing their best to look as if nothing that had happened here was of any concern to them. Gander smiled when she saw me emerging into the edge of the clearing with Ring beside me. She leaped up like a child happy to see its parents home at the end of the day, but when she came closer, she snarled, "This never would have happened if you had been here." It would have happened no matter what, but I only said, "How is that so?" She pouted and said she did not know, but that it was so all the same. That is the sort of thing I had to put up with all along. Then Linkon came to tell me what they wanted. Linkon was our translator. She was the only one who could communicate with them. I did not know how she did it, but she did it. I did not even want to know. I still do not want to know, though now, of course, it is too late for her to tell us. She told me then that they wanted their share. "Their share?" I asked her. She said that they had discussed the matter and, seeing that we were visitors, they would settle for one and let us have the other two. It was a one-time-only offer. "For what?" I asked her. Linkon shrugged: "Sometimes it is better not to know." "But *you* know," I said. She shrugged again. "Suppose we refuse?" I asked. To share the spoils, I was going to add, but I thought she might take my sarcasm too literally. She shrugged once more. "*You* suppose," she said. But already they had Desnick up on their bony shoulders and were hauling her away, trailing shrouds of pink fog. The members of the crew were chatting with each other as if nothing whatsoever was happening. Only Collins and Erickson seemed to be behaving properly. Was it really true that if I were there none of this would have happened? Did they all think that? Did the monsters? Do you?

Besides, how is it possible for one person to be everywhere at once?

Since the end of our training session, Ring had allowed her red hair to grow long again. She sat on a large rock and stared at the barbecue pit where we had prepared our feast the evening before, and chewed on her hair. "What will become of us?" she said. She stuffed fistfuls of red hair in her mouth and chewed and chewed. A pointless, filthy habit, I thought, though in fact it was just what we were all doing to ourselves. "Nothing," I told her, "nothing will become of us." I cannot understand why people are always coming at me like that, with their difficult questions, especially questions about what will happen next, especially in times of crisis, when it is all I can do to take care of myself, when I am making every effort on my own part *not* to ask difficult and unanswerable questions. What difference does it make that I was the commander of the expedition? I got the ship there, did I not? I got it back, did I not? Yet, even still, the difficult questions continue. Must I be held responsible for everything that happened in between? I did not even attend the barbecue, but what difference did that make? You chew on your fingernails. Ring chewed her beautiful hair. "What will become of us?" she said again and again. I'm not even sure it was a question any longer, but finally when I could not stand to listen to it one more time, I said, "The same thing that always becomes of us. We will die here alone. Or we will go back home and die alone."

"Oh, shut up," she said. "Who asked you, anyway?"

Desnick and Downey came back to the ship from collecting specimens of flora with what they claimed was a talking plant, but I was in no mood for frivolity by then; I only wanted them and their plant to shut up and go away. As it turned out, I need not have worried about the plant, which refused to speak in my presence, though later on, after Downey had spent the afternoon showing it around, everyone else claimed to have heard it. "What shall we do with it?" they asked. "Whatever it wants," I snapped. "Why don't you just ask it?" Never before had such looks of long-suffering indignation been inflicted upon me. I waved them away. Whatever it was they had, Downey was carrying it in a small plastic container. I did not even want to see it. I didn't want them to approach any closer. "Take it away," I told them, "and replant it where you found it. How do you know it's a talking plant? Maybe it's a vegetating talker." I was only half-serious, if that, but I could see I had alarmed them. With good reason, as it turned out. Many an inadvertent jest, I suspect, snips a peephole in reality, if only we had the good sense to look through and see what was headed our way. Meanwhile, preoccupied as I was with the matter of the unapproachability of the larger and more solid life forms, I was only concerned that they not abandon their specimen with me. "Take it to Linkon," I told them. "Let her converse with it. Or better yet, put it back in the ground and take Linkon to it." However offhandedly I said that, it was a brilliant idea in principle and, if put into practice at once, might well have saved Downey from her unspeakable fate.

But we have not come that far yet; we do not know how to put things back where they were.

# The State of the Art

After the initial shock of our arrival had worn off, we were overtaken by a general sense of amazement to find ourselves where we were. Such is the state of the art that we had merely the barest information from the unmanned probe that had preceded us: only that the planet was both inhabited and habitable. But what can a machine do, except analyze the atmosphere and take a census of the population. What does a machine know about how to live, especially in a world that is already inhabited, a world packed to the brim with others, from which others billow up everywhere, like smoke, like mist, like clouds. I don't know what we expected, actually: perhaps deserts, sandstorms, brutal heat by day and bone-cracking cold by night, raging carnivores and howling winds, violent savages and demented technocrats. Even such a world as this operates on a far more subtle level than that. The air felt thick and pleasantly warm, sweet and tart together, and slightly—what was it Schwartzie said?—"like a lemon that had been squeezed and left to sit in the sun." The ground was moist without being wet, firm and spongy at the same time. Flora and fauna abounded, in an amazing proliferation of forms, as great as Earth's own plentitude. If, among ourselves, we referred to some of the larger creatures as monsters, it was only because they did not fit any of our preexisting categories. It was merely a term that we amused ourselves with, for they kept a curious and respectful distance from us at all times and never made a threatening gesture. In spite of what has been said, I cannot believe that Linkon would have shared our private little joke with them, but we will never know. Perhaps they lacked a sense of humor. To be sure, their world seemed serious enough in all its profusion. Even the pink, cotton-candy clouds, which should have been laughable, props from a Disneyland version of an alien planet, seemed to be feeling their way about as if on some important mission. There were so many creatures, of all sizes and shapes, to say nothing of the plants. How was one to deal with so many . . . things? Whom was one to address oneself to, especially when the monsters turned out to be so unresponsive? If their world was lush and beautiful, it was also too much. We were prepared to negotiate with *someone*, not with everyone, not with all these others. There are always so many others, it is always such a problem, it must have been a problem even in Eden. And meanwhile, Harrison was wandering about interrupting us all at our assigned tasks and exclaiming over and over again, "Where *are* we! I can't b*elieve* this place!" He wanted to have a party right away, to which we would invite everyone, everything. A giant barbecue in this lovely pink weather and this lush and beautiful out-of-doors. He was very, very insistent, and soon had worked up considerable enthusiasm among the crew, in spite of my warning that we did not yet know the difference between the edibles and the invitees.

It seems to me that we spend much of our lives quibbling over one thing and another but are poorly prepared for making the truly crucial distinctions.

We were, as I am sure you can recall, a multiethnic crew. "O Brave New World!" the newspapers headlined as we prepared for departure. Multiparanoid, I might have added, since they were bickering right up to the very last moment about whether to add one more black or yellow skin to the crew, one more Catholic or Jew. I do not think it would have made any difference, however, if we had been a crew of clones. Who was it named our ship *The Caliban*? There was nowhere we could have landed where each and every one of us could not have said, "I do not think they have seen the likes of us here before." Here, suddenly, *we* were other, all of us. Needless to say, a great deal of tension accompanied us on our landing, not altogether unlike that which we had lived with on the entire flight out, only a little more evident in the violent silences, the glares, the sharp, nudging elbows as we bunched together in the hatchway and prepared to descend the landing ramp. The monsters were already assembled there, waiting for us to disembark, their great pale faces appearing and disappearing as the pink clouds rolled across them. "I don't like the looks of it," said Hebb, as we paused at the top of the ramp. "I told you we are come where we are not wanted." "Do you see any weapons?" I asked, knowing there were none. "Grim," she said, "very, very grim." "In what way grim?" I demanded. It was time to get going; we could not pause at the moment of our arrival forever. "Just look at those faces," she said, "if that's what they are." Even among our own kind, I wanted to tell her, we have not yet learned to read the face of another, but we could not stand here quibbling endlessly on the brink of this historic moment. At last we started down the ramp. I was the only one speaking by then, urging our little parade on from the rear with a little lighthearted banter in an attempt to revive our spirits. "Let us call this place Setebos," I said, in an undertone, "at least until we know that's its real name." I alone of the entire crew was aware that that was the way Mission Control had been referring to it all along. I was about to step off the ramp and move forward through the crew to make my formal greeting to the assembled monsters, when Scales stopped abruptly right in front of me, blocking my way. "Uh oh," she said, "I don't think they're ready to cope with black folks here."

She turned back past me, ducked under the ship, and was never seen again.

No sooner had we seen Earth disappear from sight on the journey out than the crew, one by one, began to come down with a variety of skin ailments: boils, rashes, hives, eczema. They came knocking on the door of my quarters to show me the scaly patches on their legs and the oozing pustules on their backs. I myself was bothered by some generalized itchiness, but no doubt that was merely caused by the dryness of the on-board atmosphere. I do not mean to complain, especially at this late date when most of their conditions have been alleviated in one way or another, but I tell you, we had hardly lifted off when things began to break out all over. I suppose that is the way it always is, especially when you are saddled with the responsibility of leadership. But skin conditions! Hebb was standing in my doorway, scratching. "I'm sorry," I said, "but I can't help you." "It's not that," she said. She had her fingernails buried deep in the flesh of her forearms. "Well then?" I asked, a little impatiently, I am sorry to say, since I had some scratching of my own I wanted to get on to. But someone has to maintain a sense of propriety. She looked up at last from raking her nails across her arms and said, "I think we have come where we are not wanted." Over the ensuing months she played a great many variations on that theme, more than I would ever have dreamed were possible. To be the leader of an expedition does not, I assure you, mean that you are able to foresee all possibilities. Perhaps that is just as well. What good could it have done me to have known that a day out, less than a day out, the entire crew would be preoccupied with looking out for their own skins: white, red, black, brown, yellow, splotchy, broken-out. . . . "Sir?" said Hebb. I had not realized she was still standing there. Perhaps I had not realized it was a question she had posed. I was anxious to inspect the mole above my heart, which I suspected of having begun to grow larger. Apparently more time passed. There were red furrows on Hebb's forearms, and she was chattering, "Not wanted. Not wanted." Months later I would find her huddled beneath a bush, chattering, "Want to go home. Want to go home." For now, however, I attempted to placate her by explaining that we had not come anywhere yet, that so far we were only in the vast and empty reaches of space, which would become vaster and emptier yet as we passed beyond our solar system.

"Precisely," she said, pointing a bloody finger at me, "and this is only the beginning."

It was such a hopeful beginning, really: the hopes of an entire world behind us, united for the first time in all of human history. Who would have missed the enveloping media coverage, the unbelievable fanfare, even the speeches? Right up to the moment we entered the ship and closed the hatches, we kept receiving telegrams, including one from my mother and another from the mayor of my hometown, on behalf of all its citizens. Do not blame them, do not even connect them with what happened; it was merely a gesture of goodwill such as everyone was offering. Nothing is connected with anything else. Things happen, that's all. We had been so carefully selected, screened, and tested and trained and trained again. We were ready for anything, for everything. Not for this apparently. Not even with four billion people crying out

# The State of the Art

"Bon voyage!" as we counted down to ignition and lifted off on the first human attempt to visit a planet that our unmanned probes had reported as inhabited. "Goodbye, Mother," I whispered at the controls as I felt the ship's power surge beneath me, "thank you for whatever it was you did that made this possible for me." Such an odd thing to say. It's just as well she couldn't hear me; she would only be turning it against herself by now, and what's the point of that? It was only that we had thought for so long that we were ready for this. Space travel was our way, contact with others our goal, the state of the art such, we felt, that we only awaited the opportunity. And now it had come. The great ship rose swiftly from the launching pad, but somehow, even as it rose, our hearts fell. All of us in the forward cabin watched the monitor intently as Earth fell away to a tiny blue and green and white ball behind us. Soon, when the tiny dot on the screen was no longer worth paying attention to, we found ourselves looking at each other. Already I could see suspicion flashing from eye to eye. It was as if leaving all those billions behind us had only sharpened our awareness, our fear if you will, of the fact that there were others to deal with now. Unknown others. And such a long journey we faced together, to begin with. Dealing with others is always hard. But what choice do we ever have? The first to break the silence on our outward journey was Ring. She unfastened her safety harness and drifted away over us in free-fall, paddling toward the cabin door. "I've got to get out of here," she said.

Such is the state of the art.

# II. Position

# Δq

After a while I could no longer tolerate the taste of just-cooked food. Only leftovers were bearable—and eventually, as to these, the longer they had been around, short of spoiling, the better. I was not averse to scraping off a little green mold. Botulism? It was a small enough risk. Nothing excited my appetite more than opening the refrigerator and finding scattered ungraciously about its shelves the remnants of three or four of last week's meals in a variety of plastic containers and serving bowls, some covered and some not, bits of meat and vegetables wrapped in plastic bags, mysteries encased in silver foil, plates with untouched servings hardening on them . . .

Perhaps it all began long ago when I first discovered my preference for Jello at that two-day-old stage when it hardens into a rubbery texture around the edges. Later I became acquainted with the pleasures of the cold carrot from last night's pot roast. Eventually the clump of congealed rice, the noodles cemented together with brown gravy. I'm not just talking about the slice of leftover ham that turns up on a sandwich in your lunch pail. I am speaking of Wiener schnitzel, scalloped potatoes, broccoli with hollandaise sauce, but always yesterday's, the day before yesterday's, last week's . . .

---

The delta q of the title refers to the uncertainty or inexactness in the measurement of the position of a particle. According to the Heisenberg Uncertainty Principle, the product of $\Delta q$ and $\Delta p$, the uncertainty in the momentum of the particle, cannot be less than Planck's constant, $h = 6.63 \times 10^{-27}$ erg seconds. In effect, the Uncertainty Principle postulates an experimentally verifiable limit to the accuracy with which one can observe and describe the universe. Science thus supports something that most writers have long suspected: there is a limit to man's knowledge. (A. Truman Schwartz)

Soon nothing revolted me more than a freshly cooked hamburger. Give me instead a cold burger discovered in plastic wrap at the back of the refrigerator shelf a week later and liberally doused with catsup, or half a slice of ancient meat loaf, a hunk of rare sirloin wrapped in foil by some miraculous savior—saver—a bowl of peas and mushrooms, the forgotten cup of chocolate pudding someone couldn't finish last Sunday . . .

In the supermarket I began to shop with my mind on leftovers. No longer did I think how good a fresh leg of lamb would taste, but only how I could dice up the leftover meat for a nice curry or serve it with bulgur wheat, noodles, rice. A rump roast divided itself up into hot roast beef sandwiches, stroganoff, chow mein. Cold mashed potatoes make marvelous little fried patties. Think of chicken: croquettes, a la king, casseroles, sandwiches, soups . . .

"Are you interested in other kinds of leftovers as well? Fabric remnants? Remaindered books? Used cars? Last place teams made up of rejects from the rest of the league? Factory seconds? Literary allusions?"

Perhaps *leftovers* is the wrong word. I prefer to think of history, which leads us to where we are, through which we come to know where we are. In the supermarket I began to shop with my mind on history. The fresh leg of lamb, the rump roast, the sack of potatoes, the plump fryers all existed as the past already. As I plucked them from the counters and dropped them into my shopping cart, I could readily see their moment of being just-cooked and freshly served as brutish and short, soon over, while their existence as leftovers—as history—was only about to begin. With leftovers you know where you are. Only in their past did they provide, for me, any sense of presence. A good shopper could get a head start by purchasing day-old bread. In the produce section there was always a cart filled with wilted lettuce, grapefruit that had begun to show soft spots, yams going bluish green at the tips . . .

I did my shopping at a run-down market in the ghetto, led there by a righteous and crusading consumer article that

Delta q

pointed out how stores in ghetto areas got poor quality food-
stuffs, cuts of meat rejected in suburban supermarkets, produce from the West Coast that has suffered from shipping
delays and failures of refrigeration. The ghetto itself is history, of course, leftover real estate passed on to its present
residents, the Mexican-Americans, from its previous residents, the Blacks, just as it had been passed on to the Blacks
by the Jews, to the Jews from the French, to the French from
the Anglos. Fresh, it had no value to speak of—a piece of
burned-off prairie where Indian hunters camped from time to
time; only as a leftover—not exactly what any of them had
cooked up—was it ever serviceable to any of these groups. I
entered it on my weekly shopping trips with all the respect—
and fear—with which Schliemann entered Troy. A world of
dented canned goods, stale sweet rolls, ground beef turning
brown, shriveled ears of corn . . .

"So your interest in leftovers—history as you call them—
was as much sociological as pathological. Eating old food allowed you to identify with the deprived sector of society, relieved you of some of the guilt inherent in your own class
position. Did you also consider buying used tvs, driving a
rusted-out, old pickup truck, finding your clothes at the
Goodwill? Did you ever consider eating in one of the mission
soup kitchens or sleeping under the railroad bridge?"

Perhaps history is also the wrong word, merely another
inadequate metaphor for the search for where things are. I
am not interested in metaphor. I am interested in things as
they are. I am interested in leftovers as leftovers. What they
are. Just as I am interested in fresh food as leftovers. Are or
will be. And leftovers I can take *as* leftovers, no need to sauce
them up and pretend they're something else. Are or will be
or have been. The reality of the leftover—a fine word once it
has been cleansed of the pejorative, freed from flights of
metaphor, washed by history. My refrigerator is full of reality:
ham and scalloped potato casserole, lentil soup, turnips,
creamed carrots . . .

*Leftovers!* For some time I had been on the verge of turning
this word over to the Maladicta Society, that branch of the

Center for the Study of Verbal Aggression that does its best, so I have been led to believe, to reveal what language is doing to our reality, to us. This was right up their alley, I would have thought: a word that was brutalizing and demeaning our reality, a perfect example of verbal agression against the world that was, at the same time, clearly self-destructive, since the world to which it referred was the world of food, the world we depend upon for our very survival. Let them see what they could do about it. I, for one, was getting tired of the way my family looked at me at the end of a meal when I started explaining to them what we could do with the leftover spinach, the leftover fillet of sole . . .

"It suddenly occurs to me that what we are really dealing with here is leftover literature. Are you not, in fact, merely a pale, warmed-over version of Kafka's Hunger Artist? Isn't it likely that if you had only found . . . ?"

Now we are getting somewhere. Your questions, of course, are nonsense. I had no trouble whatsoever finding things to eat, things I liked to eat, satisfying things, perfectly satisfying foods, as satisfying as anything at Simpsons or the Four Seasons, I dare say, and all right in my own refrigerator. I was in absolutely no danger of starving to death. If anything, I believe I was putting on weight at a rather startling rate, at least for an ordinarily thin person such as myself. Even my general health had shown considerable improvement: muscle tone, skin color, posture, gums. There is a remarkable vitality in leftovers. My fingernails no longer broke at the slightest excuse. And all this after I had entered what I am fond of referring to as my decadent period, which is to say that the nature of my leftovers had become increasingly, shall we say, sophisticated. No more cold corned beef and cabbage. An end to the catsup-smeared half of a cold hamburger. Chicken paprika was a bare minimum. I have no intention of going into all these complex recipes. Let me refer you, for example, to *The Plaza Cookbook*. You might consult, in particular, the entries for mousse de turbot, artichoke supreme, pheasant souvaroff, bisque of lobster . . .

## Delta q

"Just a moment ago you suggested that we were getting somewhere. What exactly did you mean by that? Was it my remark about literature that you referred to? Some chronological progression? The movement into gourmet cookbooks, your so-called decadent period?"

Yes. No. What I mean to say is, my family expressed growing resentment toward this new development. What's this? they cried when I presented them with chicken quenelles. At coulibiac de salmon they balked—What are you hiding in here? they wanted to know, What's that pastry covering up?—at sweetbreads parisienne they became quite shrill—You'd better tell us what's *in* this! they demanded—at their bowls of bongo bongo they just sat and stared, stirring dully with their soupspoons, and at the civet de lièvre they arose and left the table without so much as a word. This was not all one meal, you understand, but a progression, a growth, of many weeks, even months. They became aware, however slowly, that something was happening. Perhaps it took a year or so. What did I care? Time, which creates leftovers, was on my side. Into the refrigerator went these marvelous, complex preparations, sometimes surprisingly depleted, sometimes merely nibbled at around the edges, sometimes—later, later—quite entire, untouched. Vegetable delights—chestnuts puree, parsnips souffle—and miraculous sauces—mousseline, velouté, chasseur, au porto, bourguignonne . . .

The point, naturally, was that it *was* getting more difficult to tell what was in all those dishes. Each delicacy included some new ingredient, some exotic spice, some strange consistency or unique combination of its many parts. The primary question at every evening meal—What is it?—was always accompanied by its solemn refrain—What's in it? What's in it?—and sometimes by a pair of variations—Why don't we go out to a restaurant for a change? and, Tomorrow it's my turn to cook. For myself, it was difficult to keep my mind on the evening meal, either tomorrow's or the one I was in the midst of serving. It was to lunch that my thoughts were running—tomorrow's lunch when I would enjoy last night's moussaka à la turque, and next Monday's lunch, or perhaps even Tuesday's, when I could cut into tonight's saucisson en brioche . . .

"It's not at all clear to me that this is getting somewhere. Escalation yes, but progress no. It is merely getting more complex, and not at all clearer. You started to say something a moment ago about 'the point'?"

How do you yourself feel about leftovers?

"Well, ah, I'm never home much during the day, actually. I hardly have the occasion to. You see, my job . . . "

Just have a taste of this, won't you.

"Well, ah, I'm not actually hungry just now. I had a rather early lunch at the Brasserie just before I came over and, ah, well. Ah. Hmmm. That *is* interesting. What *is* it, exactly? I mean, I see what you mean, that's *very* interesting. What's *in* it, though? I can't quite recognize what all those flavors are, I mean, it is a bit different, not bad at all of course, just . . . different. What *is* it?"

It is the point which you were just asking about, which is, precisely, how difficult it is to tell what's in it. I thought I had reality in my refrigerator. I thought I had reality in my refrigerator. I thought . . . Yes, I thought, you will recall my saying, that reality was what I had in my refrigerator. Life was simpler then. Not so simple perhaps as when I was still eating freshly cooked foods, but I thought so. I thought I had reduced it to a pure simplicity by taking the route of the leftover, that with such simplicity I could achieve a certain . . . certainty—here was reality, you see, and here, on the other hand, was I—but I was wrong. Simplicity was not to be found in the cold hunk of meat encased in an envelope of gelatin, in the soggy vegetable under plastic, in the half-eaten slice of pie; no indeed, simplicity, if it was anywhere, was in what had just been brought fresh and steaming to the table, of which one could say, This is a standing rib roast, this the mashed potatoes, this the green beans almondine . . .

That was only marginal simplicity, of course, altogether too brief to find one's position in relation to it, quite useless. The vegetables cooled rapidly, the meat faded from sight under the expert manipulations of carving knife and serving fork, gravy drained away into the depths of the potatoes, one was soon swept away, before the momentum of such a reality, from any sense of one's self. A meal that had taken hours to pre-pare—one tries, how one tries! to be careful with one's real-ity—fled from the cook and server with unbelievable momen-tum. I was still standing, still carving my own first slice of beef, and already everyone else's plate was empty. Every-thing was happening too fast. I laid the slice of rare meat across my own plate and carefully sat down. I placed my hands on my lap and watched the meat on my plate. I do not know what happened to those around me. I watched my meat. I watched it cool; I watched the juices run from it and puddle around the edges of my plate and begin to congeal and even-tually become quite firm. At last I arose and put it in the re-frigerator. Beside it I placed the green beans, the potatoes, the gravy . . .

That was how it all began, you see. I know I've spoken of other beginnings, but those were not beginnings, those were merely inklings. This was the real beginning. This was the knowledge that when things had been in the refrigerator for a while, when they had had a chance to cool and thicken and congeal, to solidify—yes, hopefully, to solidify—then I would be able to know this reality, and hence to know my position in relation to it, to know, in effect, where I was, with a greater certainty. When it had lost its great momentum, yes. When it held still in place for me. With leftovers, I thought, I would find myself, find the world and then find myself. It would be simpler, I was sure: solid and motionless, how could it not be simpler. The boat of clotted gravy, the beans in the thickness of solidified butter sauce, the meat trapped in the congealed sea of its own juices . . .

And time, of course, time to see and touch and taste all those things as they really were, to have reality stripped of its momentum and laid out for my examination. But at lunch the next day, just as I was truly beginning to relish the sim-plicity at which I had arrived by such a simple device, I could not help being aware that certain changes had already taken place: changes in the appearance of the gravy, the flavor of the meat, the texture of the beans . . .

"What exactly did you say this *was*? I can't quite . . . I mean, I don't suppose I could trouble you for another taste, could I? Just a small . . . ah."

I'm sorry to belabor a single meal. We are a long way from that, of course. Months, years. The leftover began to lose its clarity, its simplicity, as soon as I had arrived at it. I had it fixed in time, more or less, but no sooner had I done so, than it began, subtly, to elude me in its place, in the very solidity of its reality that refrigerating it had achieved. The simple fact was, things no longer tasted the same! The rib roast, for example, no longer tasted, by the second day, like rib roast. Oh, it was beef, of course, just not the *same* beef. Once it had stilled and taken its place in the refrigerator, among the leftovers, it could have been *any* beef. You wouldn't believe how much I'd paid a pound for that roast, and it . . . Something had happened. It was just a piece of beef. Its clarity of outline, as it were, its distinctiveness, had blurred. It was not far from that—not that particular piece of meat, of course, but others like it, others unlike it, which I encountered during the months that followed in the same place, always in the same place—not at all far from that, I realized, not far from thinking it, tasting it as, any old piece of beef, to taking it for lamb or chicken or pork or fish or turkey . . .

It was then, naturally enough, that my cooking took the more Byzantine turn that I have already described, much to the regret of my family. It was a logical act, nonetheless. The more elaborate the dish, I reasoned, the more complex the seasonings and preparation, the more distinctive the place it would finally assume. A flawless concept. But wrong, as it turned out, utterly wrong. Momentum increased, first of all. People came to the table, looked at what was there with some care, with considerable dismay, poked and prodded, tasted, cried out, left. There were meals at which everyone was gone before I myself sat down; meals at which dishes were waved away before I'd even set them on the table; dishes, for that matter, that went straight from the oven to the refrigerator.

## Delta q

Lost in the midst of such a whirl of momentum, of meals quickly over before they had properly begun, I expected to find myself, needless to say, in the security and stability of the leftovers, in the coolly positioned timelessness of the curry, the puree, the consomme, the mousse . . .

"Is it a *mousse*? Is *that* what this is? I don't think I ever would have guessed it. Are you quite sure?"

It was not to be, of course. Perhaps you'd better have another taste, much good may it do you. Much good did it ever do *me*. The greater the culinary complexity I brought to bear on these leftovers, the more the sense of their reality began to elude me. Here, you may as well take the whole bowl. Haven't we been taught that the more information is brought to bear on something, the greater the level of certainty we can attain? Oh, I brought information to bear on those dishes all right, all the information in my kitchen it seemed at times, every spice, every mixing bowl, every utensil . . .

"Mmmm, *not* a mousse, I think, after all. Perhaps . . . "

I only wanted to be comfortable with my reality, you understand. To know it, for what it was, and to take my own place beside it. Yes, try that one there if you like. Haute cuisine let me down. Very simply, the more complex the dish, the less identifiable it soon became as a leftover. Here's a clean spoon if you think it'll help. Nothing really helps, of course, not even labeling the bowls, in the long run. I begin to think it is the nature of this reality, which is clearly not so simple as I had once assumed. The more complex it becomes—or reveals itself as being—the less we are able to know it for what it is. All those spices together, all those ingredients that must be in there, who can distinguish them? Help yourself, a refrigerator full of gourmet concoctions that have all within a few days, a week perhaps, not much more, come to taste alike, or if not actually to taste alike, then to become equally unidentifiable. A leftover hamburger was a leftover hamburger, but an ancient mousse, if that is what this is—here, do you want to try it?—is anything. I myself can no longer place it. If I cannot place it, how, where, can I place myself? Perhaps it is the mousse, who knows—there's a mousse in here somewhere—it might just as well be that one as any of these others. Watch your dripping there. Perhaps it's this one, though. Does this look like a mousse? I know there was a mousse in here somewhere. If you ate them all, you would be sure to have eaten the mousse. A statistical certainty. Is that any help? I myself do not believe there is any succor in statistics. I do not want to know that I have eaten the mousse; I want to know that I am eating the mousse while I am *eating* the mousse. Only then will I know where I am instead of merely where I have been. No no, you go right ahead; I don't think I'm hungry just now. I am hungry for certainty, that is all, for a small taste of certainty. Do you think that's the mousse, then? All I want is a moment now and then when I can say, This is I, this is reality, we are face to face and it is known what we are. Where we are. I cannot go back to the cold hamburger; the hamburger will disappear in a whirl of momentum, devoured before it can truly become a leftover. The still world, on the other hand, is incredibly complex, positioned in unidentifiable complexity. What is one to do? Perhaps that one *is* the mousse, after all, what do you think? No, that one. Say something. This one?

# Leanings

Hunched over to protect themselves from the rain, everyone leans in toward the grave. I lean with them. From the grandfathers, I am thinking, we inherit this tilt toward death. The death is theirs, the tilt ours. From the fathers comes something else—some resistance to this tilt, I suspect, some drive, some force like that which instructed me how to dress for this ceremony, how to stand up straight and keep my mouth closed. But it is the grandfathers, I am beginning to understand, whom we watch in their deepening involvement with death, watch ever so closely, until we begin to lean in toward them ourselves: a tilt that—like color blindness, left-handedness, artistic talent—seems to skip a generation, at least in this family. Such is the recognition that seeps into me, like the damp chill that rises through my thin-soled "good" shoes as I stand in the cold November rain, listening to the intonations of death. I want to whisper something—anything—into the ear of my attractive cousin, but she is on the opposite side of the grave, between her own parents. The rain has blurred my glasses so badly I can't even make out her features. Is she crying? Am I? Perhaps afterward, at the funeral feast, I can touch her.

We leave the cemetery in my father's car, grandmother sandwiched between father and mother in the front seat, brother and I in the back. Grandmother keeps sucking in her breath as if to begin saying things, but then exhales in slow silence, her sentences disappearing silently into the humid interior. The ventilating system hums softly, easing us with warm air, dispelling our moisture drop by drop. Brother is enormously proud of the fact that we do not have to depend on the funeral parlor's Cadillac because we have our own. It is a purple Cadillac. Nestled in one corner of its wide back-seat, I am busy trying to muffle my sneezes. I am sure I have caught something terrible at the cemetery.

The funeral feast, though by no means the first I have attended, remains a great mystery. The thing I feel I have to solve at it is: Where is death? Not a clue can I find among these happily chattering relatives. I approach my father, who stands among them in the center of the living room, to ask him why they do this. You remember my cousins from Richmond, he says to me. Indeed I do. She is the most beautiful woman I have ever seen. She reminds me of Rita Hayworth, and I have dreamed about her continuously since the last funeral feast. He is equally handsome, tall, just slightly balding. The two of them could have walked right off a movie screen into my aunt's living room. He is a mechanic and she, a waitress. When she says, Hello, Sonny, how are you?—using a nickname I thought I had throttled years ago—I cannot respond coherently. Lust and rage are doing battle over my tongue. I do not know how I am. I think about how she must be, under her dress, and I sneeze.

My cousin is nowhere to be seen. For a moment, I glimpsed her carrying things to the dining room under her mother's instructions, saw her slender form passing back through the hallway toward the kitchen. But now the kitchen contains only the black maid brewing coffee, and the dining room table is surrounded by relatives, my cousin not among them. I cannot even make my way through the dining room, which is crowded with relatives three and four deep between the buffet, which is stacked with plates and silverware and cups and saucers and glasses, and the dining table, which is filled from end to end with platters of food: sandwich trays, bowls of pickles and olives and celery, loaves of sliced bread, rye and sesame rolls, platters of cold meats—corned beef, roast beef, tongue, pastrami—bowls of salad, condiment bottles, cherry tomatoes, deviled eggs, a mound of chopped liver. On the sideboard at the far end of the room, almost hidden behind the massed bodies of these relatives who have come together today from half a dozen states, who are celebrating their reunion with food and talk, I can see cakes and pies, cookies and fruit. There is nothing to do here but take a plate, wedge my way in toward the table, and begin to fill it.

But I have to sit to eat, lest I should sneeze again, this time with a plate precariously balanced in my hand. I am by no means sure enough of what goes on at these occasions to risk making a spectacle of myself. It is, of course, my cousin with whom I would prefer to eat, but since she is nowhere to be seen and I cannot chance wandering about too long with this overloaded plate, I end up sitting on the floor at the far end of the living room, at my uncle's feet, within sight of my grandmother now. She is seated just across the room, a barrier reef of relatives, not all of whom I recognize, both sitting and standing around her. She holds only a cup of coffee in her hand. She holds her chin up and looks very regal. Perhaps my uncle, my father's brother, can explain the mystery here to me. He has always treated me as a favorite, though with my grandmother he seems to share the remarkable talent for making each of us—each grandchild, niece, or nephew—feel like the favorite. Therefore, there is no end to our arguments over which of us actually *is* the favorite. But he was the first to acknowledge my abandonment of my nickname, the only one, to my recollection, who has never once slipped back into using it. I give him special credit for helping me across that difficult transition to the impossible stage I now find myself in. And therefore, no doubt, special responsibility for helping me on.

So I ask him: What's this all about? That's not my real question, of course. My real question is: Why, if this is a funeral, am I enjoying myself so much? I don't think I ever realized before that there were so many good-looking women in this family. And everyone seems to be having *such a good time!* I look up at him earnestly, a kaiser roll stuffed with chopped liver in my hand. He has a highball in his. He has been discussing business with my other uncle, my father's sister's husband, seated next to him, also with a highball in his hand. Well, they ask in unison, how do you like all these relatives? New people are coming in the door all the time. I see my father rising to greet them, helping with their coats and hats. My grandmother nods to acknowledge their appearance. All these relatives? It is an overwhelming question, and my uncles can readily see that I am beyond my depth. Between them, they come to the conclusion that all the other nieces and nephews must be in the den, watching television. It is the first set in the family.

Brother and numerous insufferable younger cousins have indeed occupied the den. They are lined up on the couch like birds in the limbs of a tree, perched not just on its cushions but on its arms and back as well, all staring silent and open-mouthed at the television set fitted into the bookcase on the opposite wall. Around the room, on little metal trays set on metal folding stands, are scattered the remnants of the food they have brought in with them. On the television set, on the single channel yet available, two burly wrestlers take turns lifting each other into the air and slamming each other to the mat. Their grunts and thumps are the only sounds in the room, save for occasional scuffling sounds from the couch, signs of an unspoken battle for position. It is an explosive situation, and the cousin I am looking for is not here.

My mother's brother intercepts me in the hall outside the den, looking for my mother. Not really a part of this family, he needs her, I quickly understand, for security, to get through this ordeal of paying his respects. For this kindly, curious diabetic, I have long been aware, all social situations, no matter how small their scope, are an ordeal. For all the frequency of his visits to our house, so brief are his stays that I am sure I have not seen him for a total of more than a few hours in my entire lifetime. Perhaps he knows something about the nature of family that will help me to understand what is happening here. Do you know what's going on? I ask him. I just stopped in for a minute to see your granny, he says, I got to be moseyin' on, where's your mother? His question reminds me that I have not seen her myself since we arrived. I was just looking for her myself, I lie, happy to have some company, however silent, on my own quest, aware that I too could do with a little security.

# Leanings

It is my father we find instead, standing in the kitchen doorway. You remember my cousin the professor, he says. I do: I will undoubtedly have him as a teacher if I go to the University next year; he is famous for an annual demonstration in which he hypnotizes his entire introductory psychology class. Out of the corner of my eye, I notice my uncle moseying on in search of my mother. He does not know what to do with his cigar. Where's your cousin? the psychology professor asks me. The house is full of cousins, but we both know which one he's talking about. He is showing off, demonstrating his mind-reading act, but I suddenly discover that I have one too. It tells me that if he finds her, he will put his arm about her, whisper into her ear. I haven't seen her, I tell him, truthfully as it happens. Next year she and I will sit together in his class, side by side, in the last row, daring him to hypnotize us. For a moment, when I first walked up to him and my father, I was thinking, here is the perfect man to explain this curious scene, this joy in death. But already, in his presence, my view of the joy has dimmed. What I see is his small wife standing behind him, her plate filled with olives, both pimiento-stuffed and ripe, black ones.

As the afternoon passes, the crowd of relatives is swollen by an influx of close friends of the family. They do not eat, but eddy about my grandmother's chair, then drift away to talk briefly with the relatives they know best, then depart. I can see that they have other visits to make. My mother I have finally found seated beside my grandmother, quietly cheerful, and for a while I go and stand behind the two of them, equally quiet, until I become bored by the introductions. I have met all these friends before, I do not care to meet them again, I do not remember their names; they are a somber lot, by no means so attractive as the members of my own family. Late afternoon tiredness creeps over me; my eyes grow heavy. In the dining room the maid is clearing the ransacked platters of food from the table. The center of gravity has shifted to the sideboard, with its coffee urn, its apples and oranges, a few remaining slices of cake, several different kinds of cheese barely touched. An aunt, her back to me, opens the den door, peers in, closes it without a word, then turns away and tries the door beside it, which is closed and locked: the bathroom door. It stands just opposite the stairway to the second floor.

So I finally discover my cousin alone in her room upstairs: the closed door a sure sign of her presence. I knock, identify myself, then enter at her invitation, closing the door softly behind me. She has her back to me. She is kneeling in the love seat in front of the window, the curtains drawn back, looking out into the backyard. The room is almost dark; there is not a light on. I approach the love seat and kneel on its cushion, lean forward to look out with her, and see the rain still streaming steadily down. Across the yard is another, newer house, the doctor's I think I have been told, brightly lit in the dusk. In the yellow glow of its kitchen, almost directly below us, a woman is moving about in front of the window. I reach over and undo the top button on my cousin's blouse and slip my hand inside, squeeze against her bra, then dip inside the bra to hold her small, soft breast. Her own hand rises to press mine in place. After a while, her other hand comes to rest on my thigh. But we do not look at each other. We lean together and look out at the rain and the kitchen window, where the woman appears, disappears, reappears.

# Myopia

The story they still tell in the family is that when I got my first pair of glasses, at age four, I was so enamored of them that I refused to take them off even when I went to sleep. A pudgy child—I have seen what are purported to be photographs of me from that era, and though they are badly focused and faded with age, the plump thighs and arms, the general softness, almost shapelessness, are still apparent—as just such a pudgy child, then, I am supposed to have waddled off to bed clutching the wire rims of my spectacles tightly to my puffy little face and firmly resisting all parental efforts to remove them. And who can blame me? Who is there who doesn't want the world to be a sharp, clear, well-focused, and hard-edged place, instead of the fuzzy and ill-defined thing it really is?

But it's amazing how sight rules the senses and how what we see is what we're told we see. How the world is ruled by the sick and deluded. But that is nothing new, and I am rushing things, anyway, letting myself get swept away from my simple little story, from myself. I once was blind, but now I see. And oh, what I see! It is indeed amazing. I am overwhelmed and hardly know how to begin. For the sake of clarity, I ought to say, let us begin at the beginning. But that is precisely the point at issue here: clarity. When I think of the things we have done for the sake of clarity . . .

For the sake of tradition, then, if not for clarity, let us try to begin at the beginning. Like everyone else, I am a refugee, a displaced person from my own childhood. A perfectly happy childhood, till age four at least. I toddled about clutching various fuzzy, stuffed animals in my plump arms. I went outside and slopped around in backyard puddles and gutter puddles and empty lot puddles and came back inside covered with mud and weeds and dog shit. I smeared my face and hands and clothes with peanut butter and jelly, I had catsup in my tangled hair and mashed potatoes in my untied sneakers and brown stains in my little white underwear, and I am not really managing to fulfill my own intention of beginning at the beginning because in fact I remember none of this because at age four—Bang!—they slapped those spectacles onto my face, they punched me in both eyes with the announcement that the world was not what I had taken it to be for those first four years, that I was deluded, I was wrong, I was probably not even having the good time I thought I was having, in fact my childhood had been miserable to date, I could not have been more mistaken, not once had I seen things right, clearly, like *this*, the way I was suddenly seeing them through my first pair of glasses, little round wire-rimmed things that clung to my face like the burrs that always clung to my clothes, that taught me how the world was supposed to be seen and thereby obliterated everything that had ever happened to me before that moment.

Time passes. It is 1951. Summer. I am eight or nine years old. I am sorry for the doubt, the leap. I can see that this story must be told in fragments. Perhaps that is the only way anything can be told now. I was trying to set this down—"Time passes. It is 1951. Summer." Etc.—when Catherine walked in and saw me with my nose pressed to the paper.

"What do you think you're doing," she quoted at me, "don't you know it's impossible to make art at the end of time?" Actually, that was a line she'd been trying to use in a story before it became impossible to write anymore.

"I am not making art," I reply. "I am only working on a little reality." By the time I say this, however, she has picked up the angora sweater she was looking for and is gone. All the same, she knows.

The letters I was struggling to make were mere blurs on the paper; that's what you see when you get your eyes this close up. The ink on the edges of the letters runs out through the fibers of the paper so that all the borders, all the edges of

# Myopia

the letters, therefore all the letters themselves, are quite fuzzy. You can see from that alone, when you get down to that tiny level where, if anywhere, it would seem that at last we ought to have a little focus, a little resolution, a certain definition, you can see right there that art is impossible. That a little reality is the best we can hope for. In whatever fragments we can manage it. With all its blurry edges.

So it is 1951. Summer. I am eight or nine years old, depending on whether it is before or after my birthday. I am a little hazy on that. I am a child of the War, born even as my father lies dying on an island in the South Pacific, run over by a U.S. Army jeep. Already the world is in fragments, again. By 1951 I have run through several fathers, and in spite of the fact that I perceive the world ever more clearly through the successively stronger lenses of the new glasses that are attached to my face each year, the concept of *father* has become quite indistinct. I cannot recall who my mother's current husband is on this particular occasion, this year or season, but it makes no difference. We are at my mother's sister's house, and as usual the father is not with us. I remember that here they had a real father around. Given the size of the house, he was not seen with great frequency, but nonetheless my regular visits here gave me a certain sense of presence that I came to associate vaguely with the notion of father, even though in this case I had to refer to him as uncle.

I remember him passing slowly across the veranda above us, indistinct in the twilight haze and the heavy cloud of cigar smoke that followed him everywhere, while Bunny and I played in the formal gardens below. I might have been nine by then. It could have been my own birthday we were there to celebrate that evening, unless it was Bunny's, which fell earlier in the summer than mine, in which case I was still eight. My birthdays were always celebrated at my aunt's, sometimes a little belatedly if we had been traveling, as was often the case during the summer months, but usually within two or three weeks of what my mother asserted to be my actual birth date. Given the vagaries of our own living arrangements, it was doubtless assumed that some sense of stability might be provided for me by annually celebrating the approximations of this event on my aunt's estate. It was fine with me; I always loved to visit there: a great rambling old place, house and grounds both, in which it was possible for a child to get endlessly lost without ever quite losing hold of safety. Christmas and birthday toys I regularly squirreled away there in unused rooms and storage closets and abandoned stairwells, but I cannot recall that I ever found any of them on subsequent visits.

And then there is my cousin Bunny, with whom I am playing in the formal gardens on this summer evening in 1951. I have never understood why they call her Bunny, for she is tall and angular, just like me. She is a collection of sharp edges: knees and elbows and shoulder blades and nose. Everything about her juts out like a dangerous weapon, and since I can see quite clearly through my new glasses the likelihood of receiving painful injury from the well-honed instruments of her body, I keep my distance from her very carefully. Nonetheless, I am madly in love with her. Nonetheless, we keep our distances, for my own body is much like hers, and it must seem to both of us that to come into any physical contact would resemble a clashing of swords. Ever since that first pair of glasses was bandaged around my face, my body has labored to define and clarify itself, to melt away the blur of baby fat and send out to the world its clear, hard images of cartilage and bone. By the summer of 1951, though you might not believe it to see me now, it has been remarkably successful. Bunny and I stand stiffly out in the garden like a pair of angular robots assembled from an Erector set and placed just far enough apart so that if one falls, the other will not be damaged. The evening darkness is rising up out of the garden and over the veranda, lapping against the sides of the great house itself, though in the lighted windows of the south wing we can see a few ill-defined figures gliding vaguely by. My mother? Probably she is on the telephone, her lucid voice ringing out over the long distance lines to her friends around the country, though as I found out when I was sent away to boarding school to become the recipient of her regular Sunday evening calls, it always emerged from the other end slightly garbled. And Bunny's parents? In a few minutes one of the adults, more likely one of the servants, will appear on the veranda, framed in the light of an open doorway, and we will hear ourselves being summoned in.

"Catch me," says Bunny, turning and running off, instantly swallowed up by the darkness and the secrecy of the garden hedge.

The hedge is not a maze, though we have often pretended that it is. But it is thick, almost as solid as a wall, and carefully trimmed; lengths of it define the perimeter of the garden, line its paths, intersect with and partition off its many flower beds. Except in a few places, it is too dense to see through even in daylight, so that playing hide-and-seek around it has always been one of the favorite pastimes of my childhood visits here. But we have never tried to play at this in the dark before. I plunge into the depths of the garden with no idea where Bunny has fled, racing recklessly along the flagstones, trying to maintain my bearings by keeping my arm stretched out to my right, in constant contact with the dense wall of the hedge where it borders the path. I hear Bunny's giggle from diagonally across the garden. She is just my age and height, but has always been able to outrun me; she does not wear glasses, and I think, turning down another darkened path, one I hope will carry me across the garden, she may well be able to see in the dark. She laughs again, much closer now. I stop. I feel from the hedge that I am at one of the rare spots where it is not so dense, and I think from her laugh that Bunny may be no further away than the other side of this hedge, so I duck my head and butt my way quickly through it, emerge into the darkness on the other side, pausing, sensing she is right there somewhere close by, but also that something else has happened. I have lost my glasses! With or without them, I cannot see a thing in this inky darkness that has now flooded over the entire garden, but nonetheless, I do not have them! They have been stripped from my face during my dive through the hedge, and now I stand here in the darkness feeling quite naked, lost, missing something very . . . very necessary.

Though I know even then that it is melodramatic of me, I cannot help wondering, for a moment, what will become of me. The only thing I can think to do, though in fact I am no more disabled by the darkness than when I had my glasses on, is to call my cousin for help. I turn about to call her, turning toward where I thought she last was, and just in the midst of that turn I bump into her.

Suddenly I understand why they call her Bunny.

It is 1958, and Bunny and I have been, as they say in that part of the country, "doing it" for a good many years now. Ever since we have been able to, in fact. And whenever we have been together—which has not been often enough for either of us, being limited to such family occasions as birthdays and holidays and subject to the whims of my mother's travels and marital state. At sixteen Bunny has not exactly become voluptuous yet, and I myself possess a sunken chest unrivaled by even my scrawniest classmates, that handful of undernourished boys dragged up from the city every year to nourish our own sense of good fortune, lest we grow fat and sloppy feeding on our complacency. Not me, though. Not Bunny either. In one of our favorite spots, the abandoned attic playroom where we lie entangled on the dusty, blue shag rug, the casual onlooker, god help us, could never distinguish my scrawny legs and knobby knees from Bunny's. We can hardly see the difference ourselves.

Here, however, there are no casual onlookers, and, glasses off, everything is done by feel. Bunny, too, has been wearing glasses for several years now, ever since the belated discovery of her astigmatism. Her parents, furious, have dragged her relentlessly through the offices of the best ophthalmologists in the country, demanding to know why this crucial defect has escaped their notice through all the years of annual checkups. I had never seen my aunt raise her voice in anger before, but now at the dinner table she rages continuously about this disaster, while my uncle slowly vanishes behind clouds of cigar smoke. Bunny herself exhibits no particular interest, except for a mild concern about whether or not to get contact lenses. Meanwhile, our glasses lie on the chess

# Myopia

set on the small table over our heads, their bows as tangled as our legs. Bunny's face is a soft blur above mine. Her body is a soft blur floating through mine. Where, we wonder quietly, have all the hard edges gone, the sharp protrusions of elbow, hip, and rib? When we lie like this, we always take the time to remind each other—it is as much a part of our ritual as the order in which we remove first our glasses, then our clothes—of that first time we bumped together in the garden, reached out to each other for balance in that shattering moment, and then fell, clinging, into the hedge, into the surprising softness of our child bodies. I had a brief image at that time of the Easter bunnies we had fondled in years past, and how quickly those soft little creatures had been plucked from our hands and returned to their hutches for, we were told, the sake of their own health and safety. Even then we lay there in the hedge for only a moment, stunned, overwhelmed, before the call came drifting down from the veranda, a clear, unwelcome voice invading our leafy darkness. And then, as we helped each other up, not daring to say a word, my hand, reaching out to the hedge for support, grabbed not branches but the cool, waiting, wire bows of my glasses.

1958, yes. I have been graduated to tortoise-shell frames. Now I not only see the world better, but I look better in the eyes of the world. I can remember the optometrist saying, as he clamped the new glasses onto my face, "There, very sophisticated now. Very mature."

He made a last set of minor adjustments with screwdriver and pliers, wiped them clean, and handed them back to me. With both hands, to show him I knew the proper way, I raised them up and submitted my eyes to their already familiar grip. The world I had come to know sprang magically into view again in all its much-touted clarity, and I stared at it—at the optometrist's knobby face, at his plasticized card of shrinking print, at my own face in his three-paneled mirror and my mother's face perched just beside me—with all the gullibility of a country bumpkin being touted the eighth wonder of the world in a carny peep show. For the sake of just such a marvel as that, it seemed I was always clasping my glasses to my face, even before I reached to turn off the scream of the alarm in the morning, sound being far less a concern than sight; with the long, scrawny arm that preceded me out of the shower, never mind that they were too steamed up to be of any practical use; from various perches around Bunny's house, not only the shelf of dolls over her bed and the ball-return receptacle of the pool table in the game room, but even a niche in the hedge again one moist and exceptional autumn night. I can remember my entire life, until only recently in fact, as a never-ending succession of attachings of endless pairs of glasses to my face: three identical pairs on this particular visit to the optometrist, for my mother, brought up on tales of Teddy Roosevelt charging up San Juan Hill with his saddlebags packed with extra pairs of spectacles, never wanted me to risk being without these precious protectors of the necessary vision of the world.

Even now, for I have not yet found it easy to overturn that belief in the gem-like preciousness of eyeglasses on which I was raised, those three pairs, along with countless others, the very history of how I have perceived the world through the decades, lie tumbled together in the messy interior of this large desk drawer my knee presses up against as I struggle to render these murky, fragmentary remarks upon these fibrous shreds of paper on my desk top. All over, today, unused pairs of glasses, discarded but not disposed of—rimless and wire rims, tortoise shell and metal framed, lorgnettes, pince-nez, tinted and photo-gray and contact lenses, too, both hard and soft—fill the drawers of the world's desks and filing cabinets and dressers and bedside tables. Not quite yet have we truly liberated ourselves from the debilitating visions of the past.

Or, in the optometrist's perennial refrain, "It will take you a while to get used to your new prescription."

Mostly, of course, the new is just the old all over again. The optometrist steps to the glass-topped altar of his waiting room and with solemn ritual affixes to your anxious, upturned face a new set of lenses, slightly altered from the last in axis and azimuth. In an awesome display of power, he quietly, quickly,

# Myopia

overturns the precarious balance of clarity he has constructed for you over all these past years and sends you spinning off once again into the remembered and feared dismay of a mangled world, out-of-focus, blurred, and dizzying. And even as he does this, he promises you clarity, dangling you over the smoky, vertiginous pit, while he preaches balance, salvation.

"Now you know the worst," he says in effect. "Only have faith, and all will soon come right again."

And within a few hours, a few days at the most—for you do trust him, of course—his prophecy comes true. The brief headache of the unaccustomed slowly fades, and once again you walk the hard sidewalks of the world as you have come to know it, climb its sharp-edged wooden steps with one hand on the faithful iron railing, and knock firmly and confidently on the solid oak door of familiarity. Dazzled into belief by the lens grinder's sleight of hand, you do not know what shadowy, vague interiors await you.

It is 1970. I am back in wire rims. Back to my childhood? No. Everyone is in wire rims now. It is the style. Even Bunny is in wire rims, "granny glasses," she calls them, only we must not call her Bunny any longer, for we are adults. We must be firm and sure. Her name is Catherine. Not Kate or Cathy, but Catherine. Is that clear? However, she still feels like Bunny to me. We are living, if not in poverty, at least in what used to be called genteel poverty. Which is to say that we do not go hungry and even in this odd northern city where we are currently residing do not suffer from the cold; we take a few magazines and occasionally enjoy a concert or a movie, and there is a cheap Mexican restaurant within walking distance that is our particular delight. But at the same time there are no rugs on our stained wood floors or curtains to cover the soiled window shades, the landlord is disinterested in the leaky plumbing and the burned-out hallway bulbs, and the unsavory trio above us battles long and late. Needless to say, we receive neither spiritual nor financial assistance from the folks back home—or wherever my mother and her umpteenth hubby happen to be residing at the moment. We have blurred the clear and necessary lines of family connection, and therefore they have clamped blinders on to shut us off from view. The only one who seemed at all sorry to see us go was Bunny's—Catherine's—father, but then he always saw the world through the dense haze of his cigar smoke. Her mother—"irrationally," so her friends and her psychiatrist assure her—blames everything, even her husband's smoky indolence, on that past, tragic failure to uncover and remedy, at an appropriately early age, her daughter's flawed vision.

In spite of her guilt and anger, she is probably right.

These days our glasses spend the night together on a warped plywood bookshelf overhanging our bed and linked precariously to the crumbling wall by a pair of bent and rusty brackets. In the bedroom proper—for Catherine and I sleep in the living room on a fold-out couch, that most ambiguous and wonderful of furnitures—our daughter's glasses, wire-rimmed also, of course, lie alone on a similar shelf above her own bed, both day and night, gathering dust, since she refuses or neglects to wear them. Like all good parents, we have had her eyes examined regularly since infancy and corrective lenses provided the instant it was discovered they would be needed to compensate for the defects in her vision: at an age not much beyond that at which they were first inflicted upon me. But with this difference: that never, in the several years that she has had them, has she been willing to wear them with any consistency. Like our own multitudinous threats and bribes, as well as the endless admonishments of her doctors, her excuses are legion. The fact is that she rarely wears them, not even to school, and when she occasionally does, the thick lenses are so covered with dust and grime or with fingerprints, almost as soon as her mother or I take the trouble to clean them for her, that it is difficult to understand how she can see anything through them. This is not laziness or vanity. Actually the glasses look quite attractive on her, and at times she seems to enjoy wearing, almost like jewelry, an old pair of gold frames, her mother's, from which the lenses have been removed. On the contrary, I am beginning to see, it is purely an act of choice.

It was feared, threatened—nothing to do with her weak

eyesight, of course—that she might turn out to be an idiot. Actually, it appears she is something of a genius. We are about to learn a great deal from her.

Seven o'clock. A winter morning. Perhaps a year later. Catherine, after working late last night, still asleep, pillow over her head, the lump of her body almost undetectable beneath the tumbled blankets. I stand in the kitchen window, still in my pajamas, waiting for the coffee to perk, looking down upon the people gathering at the corner bus stop three floors below. Jenny, age ten, rinses her cereal bowl out in the sink and slips up close beside me, letting my arm curl around her. There is no point in inquiring whether she is wearing her glasses.

"Whatcha see, Daddy?" she asks me.

"Just all those people down there," I say, pointing with my free hand, not thinking for the moment that there is no way she can see anyone at that distance, "all those different people."

In response, she reaches up suddenly with both hands and plucks my glasses from my face. It is apparent at once, in spite of my moment of instant terror, that she is handling them with care, is not even withholding them from me, but she folds the bows and gently places them on the windowsill, points out where I was pointing only a moment ago, since I have turned to face her now, leans forward to the window herself, one hand holding my arm, says, "Look."

She is my daughter. I look. All those different people have disappeared. No, they have not disappeared, but they have blurred and gone fuzzy, they are not altogether different anymore, they are instead much the same, grayish brown but glowing, radiantly, against the snow, with the shaggy sameness that brings them together here five mornings a week.

Across the street the hard-edged sense of outline—roofs and chimneys, brick walls and wood-framed windows—fails a row of apartment buildings just like the one we live in. Above them smoke merges into gray sky. For a second it almost seems that if I were out there I could plunge my hand through their suddenly softened walls and caress the bodies of small children sleeping inside. A large red blur glides vaguely down the street and comes to a stop below us, where the gathered crowd flows like a drop of water through rapid changes of shape and then drains away into the waiting red receptacle. Other colors, other shapes, glide slowly up and down the white street, its wintry clarity suddenly turned vague and amorphous, almost warm, almost human, almost as open to the touch as, I think, the image I have as I stand there, the tactile image, of Catherine's thighs, pressed softly together now beneath the wool blankets, to which, I think, I shall soon be returning.

"Here, Daddy," says Jenny, quietly but, I suspect, a little derisively, as she hands me my glasses, reaches up to kiss my cheek. "I gotta go now. You probably need these." And I strap them back upon my face as she grabs her pile of books, purse, gloves, and hat off the kitchen table and her coat from the hook behind the door, all with unerring accuracy—it's not possible that she can see any of that without her glasses, but she seems to *know* where her world is—and hurries out of the apartment.

It is true that this can only be told in fragments: the torn pieces and shattered edges of reality, the broken leavings of a century of war; tattered remnants of the holocaust, of toppled or crumbling political systems, of revolutions in social structures, sciences, and the arts; the bits and pieces of the rending of the very fabric of human consciousness. As all the desperate futility of this past decade's outpourings of books and films, symposia and seminars, its sad, sad reassemblings of old religions and ideologies and assembly-line manufacturing of new ones, has shown us, neither a clarity of vision nor a vision of clarity has proven capable of redeeming us from this chaos. How can we not, at a time like this, and with the comfortably blurring distance of history, pity poor Spinoza, hunched up at the workbench with his grinding tools, trying to accomplish with his optics what he couldn't do with his philosophy: the bringing of the world into focus. Perhaps he was perfectly aware all the while that to do so with his lenses was just another trick of necessity, not unlike the invention of god.

# Myopia

Meanwhile, Catherine's hit-and-run accusation, however comic its intent, still rankles a bit, as perhaps it was meant to: she is not one for letting any of us forget exactly where—and when—we are. When: the present. Where: a much nicer apartment, at long last, thanks in some small part to the vagaries of the inheritance laws as well as to the success of Catherine's radio program and my own publicly funded and well-paid research work on the future of libraries. Jenny's glasses, however, still rest in a coating of dust on a shelf, a much nicer shelf to be sure, above her bed, while Jenny herself is off at college. She is not actually *at* college, but spending the year in South America, immersing herself in the translucent blur of other cultures, other languages. She will know them thoroughly when she returns, with all her senses.

I want it understood, however, that I am not making art. That I am not sitting here grinding away at the lenses of perception. That I do not succumb to the peculiarly modernist delusion that one more set of spectacles, one final adjustment of curvature, one last lucid point of view, and all will come clear. All will not come clear. This blur—this "mess" as the reactionaries like to put it, or, as some of our intellectuals prefer, this "suffusion"—is what we live with. That is what we truly know now, however many choose not to accept it and to live, still, with the old gods of perception, wrapping their faith ceremonially around their ears each morning when they awake, after they have first, furiously, tried to wipe away each speck of dust with which the relentless world has managed, overnight, to besmirch their vision. All day, out in the city now, you can see them, the young most assiduously of all, stopping on the sidewalk to remove their glasses, holding them up to the light, pulling out a Kleenex or a handkerchief or one of those chemically treated papers the drugstores sell, wiping both lenses, holding them up to the light to examine them once again, wiping one more time, in desperate pursuit of every smudge, every smear, every speck, every little thing that undermines the precarious belief in the world's clarity they still manage, in spite of all, to maintain.

For my part, I spend much of my time with the old people

these days. Yes, we are still in the present for the moment. Nothing to be afraid of, really. I have been spending a considerable amount of time riding the bus with the old people. Because of my freedom to arrange my own hours for my research work at the library, I ride the bus at odd times, not with the standing room crowds on their way to or from work, but later in the morning some days, earlier in the afternoon others. These are the hours when the elderly choose to ride also, safe from the rush-hour crushes and the harried drivers nagging them to hurry on or off. At ten in the morning or two in the afternoon they can creep aboard as slowly as they want, fumble for their change in the doorway, and still be secure in the knowledge that the bus will not lunge suddenly ahead while they are easing their way down the aisle. In mid-afternoon their arms are filled—bags from the grocery, small packages from the drugstore, parcels from friends and children, purses, hats, scarves, letters, magazines, news-papers—and relief clouds their faces as they settle heavily onto the plastic seats. Their shoulders sag and their eyes water, but as they turn their heads about, nodding and smiling at the other, familiar, aged passengers, at the driver, even at me and the stray child or two who dares to be out of school at this hour, it is clear that there is something they know. Something eases the ache in their mottled legs and the clutter of parcels slipping from their laps and the unruly scattering of white hairs dangling around their ears and over their eyes, and I think that perhaps it is a kind of wisdom to which we are all worn down at last: a growing exhaustion from the life-long effort of sustaining the myth of clarity, but an exhaustion that grows throughout the years, dully and predictably as the century plant, until suddenly, in its proper season, it blos-soms into something entirely different. Tired out by the strain of all those years of insisting upon seeing things just as we have been told they are supposed to be seen, we finally awaken, only in our decline, sad to say, to see the world as it really has been all along, just as it is revealed to us here on the bus: wrinkled and slumped, running at the eyes and drooling at the mouth and no doubt oozing from its other orifices as well, sprouting unwelcome hairs, dusty and drippy, furrowed and frazzled, covered with crumbs and splattered with stains and appallingly real.

That is my bus. That is your world. That is too much for most of us still, who label this condition senility and dismiss it from the narrow parameters of the acceptable. It is even too much for many of the elderly, untutored as all of us in how to cope with their slow, belated awakening to this true vision of the world, who flee instead to the safety of retirement villas, nursing homes, and the firm, reassuring hands of the mortician. But it is sad for all of us that we are such slow learners.

Not *all* of us, of course.

It is 1974. Spring. Monday morning and Jenny has just gone off to school and left us alone and exhausted after a long weekend of battering us with her cloudy brilliance. Brilliant because, simply, she knows so much. Cloudy because of the way everything runs together in her tangled, breathless sentences, where ideas flow easily and continually into and through one another, their wispy, shifting borders tangling like puffs of smoke.

All weekend I have been gently berating her with clear paternal logic: "Jennifer, put on your glasses for a change and I think you will have a much better view of these issues."

All weekend she has been replying with sloppy, loving, adolescent insolence: "Father, take yours off."

They and a towel are all I now have on as I emerge from the bathroom, fresh from the shower, hair still wet and tangled, to find Bunny, I mean Catherine, crawling around on the floor, on all fours, nude and unbespectacled, on the pale yellow shag rug around our bed. She is no longer the arrangement of hard planes and sharp edges I have described before. Her breasts have swelled and softened, her thighs grown fleshier, her belly slightly rounded, and even her face has filled out, maturity easing its way over the ridges of cheek and chin and jaw; she is even more beautiful and desirable than in years past. At the moment, however, she is searching for a contact lens, one of the pair she finally succumbed to after more than

141

a decade of struggling over the decision. But she has never gotten quite comfortable with them. Out of a sense of obligation, more than anything else, she wears them for a few hours a day. And only out of a sense of obligation does she now search for the one she dropped. She would far rather drop the whole matter and reach up for her glasses on the bedside table. But we look, all the same; these are *lenses*, after all.

"Wouldn't you have a better chance of finding it," I suggest, "if you put your glasses on?"

"Un unh," she mumbles, head down, breasts gently swinging, "too close."

She is right. At this distance, down on the floor beside her, my nose nearly in the rug, things blur even through my glasses. I take them off, reach up to place them carefully on the bed above me, and then, the instant I return to the search, spot it, clinging to the tasseled edge of the bedspread where it hangs down just at floor level.

"See," she says when I point it out to her. I see. She starts to reach over me for it, since I am in her way, then playfully nudges me aside, rolls me over on my back, her hand rubbing over my own softened belly, up through the hairs that cover the flesh that covers my one-time-sunken chest.

"I see," I say. She crawls gently over me, pressing her breasts softly against me, arms and legs entangling, tongues gliding around each other, bodies entering each other with all the ease and fluidity with which our daughter's ideas have been sliding into one another these past few days. Oh Bunny, Bunny. My glasses are tangled in the branches of the hedge above me, the shag rug of the past cushions my heaving thighs. How the edges crumble and everything runs together! What a blur and what a wonder!

It was difficult to get accustomed to going without our glasses at first, so hard do old myths die. But Jenny, bless her, eased us into the world, our own daughter watching carefully over our birth. She always knew, she told us, it would only be a matter of time. Quickly, quickly, I urged her, before old age overtakes us. She smiled. She had been riding the buses all

# Myopia

along. But she guided us onward, with all deliberate haste, over the brittle dread we had been taught of rigid objects, around the knife-sharp fear of edges and corners, down into the impenetrable solidity of the world. But *into* it! For it was lies, it had all been lies. She guided us, all our glasses left behind, around the apartment, through the building, into the outside world; the streets and sidewalks, the buses and subways, the stores, offices, banks, theaters, museums, parks. Not all at once, you understand. In her amazing wisdom she saw the long-delayed comprehension of adults as a viscous fluid that had to be warmed slowly to its proper flowing, not quickly overheated till it bubbled, evaporated, and suddenly disappeared. She was taking no chances; we were her great experiment, though she also solemnly assured us of her feeling that she, somehow, was ours. So, in fact, all things do ease together. So, at last, we *saw*.

I once was blind, but now I see. Yes, you may impatiently be asking—most assuredly are, in fact, if you are *reading* this—but *what* did you see?

Just this, dear friend. Just this, dear comrade-in-arms in the long campaign for some substantial beachhead—viewpoint!—on the world. Just this, around all the precise edges and unyielding densities, through all the clear and solid geometries of your perception. Just this, oh deluded and bespectacled—or ill. Just this, which I struggle here to suggest some vague image of for you, knowing full well there is no way to frame this multitude of fragments, these smoky, shifting edges of our world.

That we have been led through all the murky, interlacing mysteries of this world with chains around our eyes instead of rings through our noses. That our vision has been manacled, our very minds cast into prison behind glass bars: behind *corrective* lenses. That we have lived lives of willing confinement, not even aware how we are victimized by lenses designed to show us the world not as it truly is but only as some powerful, crippled minority demands we see it, knowing that only by so hobbling our vision can they lead us in their own direction. Yes, we have been cast into darkness by the tyranny of 20/20, and the worst of it is that we have only ourselves to blame. For we have so lusted after the El Dorado of clarity that we have gladly sold ourselves as slaves to that false ideal, willingly submitted our faces to the buckling on of blinders, sought so desperately to see what we thought we wanted to see that we have not even seen what we could. What was right in front of our noses all the time.

For it is all around us to see, in everything we encounter, that the world is not the collection of the hard and sharp, the firm and solid, that this minority of visionary ideologues demands we see it as. Perhaps they are only deluded, not truly evil, but victims themselves, misled by some strange ophthalmic disease, some congenital defect of the eye, some curious misshaping of the cornea, into an ability to see only that small part of the world that appears—merely along its surfaces, to be sure—to maintain the clarity and rigidity of their desires. But look around you and you will see, in fact, a world that is loose and disjointed, fibrous and fuzzy, soft in its centers and uncertain around its edges, fragmented, fluid, afloat, shifting, and ill-defined, unclear in its lines and uncertain in its directions, overlapping, interpenetrating, enmeshed, entangled, ensnared: everything in everything else, all borders blurred, chaotic, inseparable, and true! Just look around and see, as we have always suspected, the human shapes in trees and the animal shapes in people, the shapes shaping up in clouds and the shapes left behind in beds and chairs, the shape of the parent in the clinging child and, in the sagging form of the adult, the shape of the child. Nothing exists wholly within itself; all spreads outward, loosening its borders like our own softening and expanding flesh, like earth and air, fire and water. Nothing is separate from anything else; just blink, the physicist will tell you, and the wave becomes a particle. Blink again and the decades spill one into the other, the ambiguous borders of families, nations—the very continents—shift and surge. Just think of the wars we have fought over insignificant chunks of wasteland and remember it was not the useless land we wanted, only its imagined confirmation of our borders. We have always wanted that certainty of where our

# Myopia

borders lay: wanted it by mutual agreement if possible, but with a willingness, if necessary, to spill our blood on arid soil for its sake, just as we have been willing to sacrifice our very minds to the firm duplicity of glasses. And what more desperate evidence do we need of how weak, how frail and crumbling, how nonexistent our borders truly are?

There is nothing in our experience, no matter how large or small, that is not interlaced with holes and shredding around the edges. Close up, all matter is as porous as smoke, just the way you see it with your glasses off; and in the distant reaches of the galaxy it is the same. Within the smallest particle, still smaller particles spin, keeping great distances between themselves; and the fiery density of the sun flares out through the solar system, enveloping the most distant planets with long tentacles of plasma and the tattered edges of invisible solar winds. Yes, even the universe itself pulses relentlessly outward at its indecipherable boundaries, rushes ever inward upon its undiscoverable center. And what of your own life, its missing center and far-flung edges, shredded by time and entwined with countless other lives, long beyond your knowledge and in ways you never imagined? Now do you see?

So take off your glasses, if you dare. Or, if you are afflicted with 20/20 vision, try to find yourself a sympathetic ophthalmologist willing to prescribe a variety of corrective lenses for your pathetic condition. Take off your glasses and see around you the very same thing the electron microscope will show you: a world of shreds and gaps and tattered edges; the ragged, frayed, twisted stuff of time and matter, world and self. Take off your glasses and bring this paper close, closer still, even to where your nose presses against it, as mine does now, and you will see, as clearly as you will ever see anything in your life or need to, how this raggedy message is itself mere pretense at providing any certainty or clarity of perception: that if it was clarity you sought, poor deluded creature that you are, like all of us have been, then once more you have come to the wrong place; that even as you move closer to it, every aspect tatters and disintegrates, organization falls away into confusion and art into the fragmentation of reality, the distances between the letters lengthen, words tumble into the vast and empty spaces of the page, the letters themselves begin to shred at their edges, becoming more and more vaguely defined as you approach them, as the ink spills outward through the matted fibers of the paper, and nothing, nothing, is clear, neither your vision nor your life nor your world nor this. This most of all.

But do not be afraid.

It is 1979. Or 1980. 1983. It makes no difference. It is now. All time runs together. Ask any historian. Ask anyone. The years have no borders. Generations plunge one into the other in the blur of the decades, and all we see are the vague forms moving through the lingering cigar smoke of the past, in the thick fog rolling toward us from the future, and in the wispy haze of presence true sight reveals around us now. It is now. It is night. Do not be afraid. If I can put this all together in the dark, this loose and shapeless mass we call our world, then you can make it out in the dark. Bunny lies beside me. She sleeps, facing softly forward against my back, her body flowing into the same shape mine has assumed here in our rumpled bed, tangled with me in the midst of tangled sheets and blankets, in our tangled bodies. There are no eyeglasses on shelves or bedside tables. Her hand has come to rest between my legs, pressing gently into the soft flesh of my inner thigh. We have been one flesh. It is completely dark here now, but I see her, feel her, smell and taste her still, hear her breathing, know her presence. We are one flesh. All things, all images and meanings, flow together. Glasses gone, all pretense at clarity dissolves. No borders, no certainties, no demands. Tatters, tatters. This blur, our world. We will be one flesh. Don't you see?

# To Be or Not To Be

In any case, it is too difficult
for me, and I wish I had been a movie
comedian or something of the sort
and had never heard of physics.

*Wolfgang Pauli*

Was my father indeed an android as she charged? Did I actually come from a whole family of androids? Exactly how much attention should be paid to rumor and innuendo, to things shouted in the heat of argument? Why did I take everything she said so seriously? Was that an android characteristic? That was what worried me most of all: if my father was an android, what does that make me? What kind of world is this where it is possible to grow up thinking you are a human being, only to be told when you have reached your middle years that you are not a human being after all, that you never have been?

\*      \*      \*      \*      \*

The argument with my wife continued as follows:

"I would call you a terrible human being, except that I haven't seen any signs of humanity in you for so long I wonder if you *are* a human being. You're just like your father, that's what you are. Maybe you're an android. Maybe you're not a terrible human being but a wonderful android. You are doing the best you can with the equipment you have."

"What's that supposed to mean?"

"That clinches it; you're an android."

"Don't I have feelings like everyone else?"

"Do you? How would you know? What would you androids know about human feelings?"

"You are assuming the very point that is at issue."

"I am assuming nothing, particularly about your so-called feelings. About anyone's feelings, for that matter. About mine.

What could you possibly know about other people's feelings?"

"You have a point there. That's a major problem. That's the whole traditional philosophical dilemma concerning knowledge of other minds. But it applies to you as well as to me. To humans, as you would say, as well as androids."

"What's to know? Look at me, I am nearly out of my skin, as any fool, any android even, can see. Look at you, you are as cool as an android cucumber."

"You are not talking about feelings now; you are only talking about the external manifestations of feelings."

"Logic! I ask for feelings and I get logic! What am I going to do with logic?"

"Reason your way out of this dilemma, perhaps. What are you going to do with feelings?"

"I am going to scream, that's what I'm going to do. I'm going to scream my way out of this, even if that means I end up screaming my way into the nuthouse."

"That is a very logical possibility."

\*       \*       \*       \*       \*

Logically, once she departed screaming, I should have put the whole incident aside and gone on with whatever I was about to do before this unfortunate encounter began. Isn't that often the best way, simply to let things work themselves out? To let time take its course. Meanwhile, you could just get on with things. You could not be endlessly hacking away at each other when there were things to do, when you had guests coming to dinner in half an hour or an airplane to catch or a sick child to nurse. You just had to do what you had to do, and perhaps that was resolution enough. We had these crises from time to time, like any other couple no doubt, and fortunately without the children around today. Generally such conflicts seemed to just dissipate as time passed, so what was the need of pursuing them, of continuing to tear into each other like a couple of wild animals, of just keeping things stirred up? Is there any resolution to be had that way? Why, that could go on and on until there was no telling what you

# To Be or Not To Be

might get into. No telling what might become of you like that, and then you would have only yourself to blame, for pursuing what you should have left alone. No thank you. Surely this way is much more humane.

Somehow, though, I couldn't remember what it was I had been about to do when the hostilities flared up. She had got her barbs in fairly deep, and I could not seem to shake them free enough to go on with whatever I had been about to do. Android, indeed! If this had been last weekend, when I took the children fishing, I could have shown her where I caught one of the triple hooks in my finger and how I sucked the blood after I cut the hook out. I could have said, "See, I bleed, too; am I not human?"

But the hook that she had set deepest, because it was not the first time she had cast this one at me, was the one about my father. True, I had never thought of him as an emotional person. But "one hundred percent devoid of feeling," as she said in her fury? I don't even recall how he entered the debate. "Just like him," she said more than once, "you're just like him!" But how could that be when all my life I had gone about with the belief that I was just the opposite of him? How could our perceptions be so different as that, that she saw me as just like him and I saw myself as totally unlike? Could she be at all right? Could a man go through his whole life and still be so deluded about himself as that?

Still standing there in the middle of the living room, after her sudden and noisy departure, I could hear in my own head her answer to that.

"Not a man," she would say. "Not a man. But an android, yes."

O Father, what have you done to me?

What *am* I?

What are *you*?

\*      \*      \*      \*      \*

Evidence on behalf of the android theory:

1. My father was the soul of perfection behind the wheel of an automobile, though I suppose *soul* is an inappropriate term in

this category. At any rate, he maintained a correct and steady speed, he stayed in his lane at all times, he did not rant and rave at other drivers, he never had an accident or received a citation for a moving violation. He lavished on his car the devoted attention that others reserve for their own grooming.

2. He was a flawless gin rummy player. Many a time I stood at his elbow and watched him in his silent concentration. The moment he picked a card, he saw every possibility for its use either in his own hand or in his opponent's. He reorganized his hand with lightning rapidity. He remembered every card in the discard pile. These same skills served him equally well at bridge, though he was far less successful at that game because he had his own bidding system, which was not the same as anyone else's bidding system.

3. He never lost his temper. Or rather, I never saw him lose his temper or heard, from anyone else, reports of his losing his temper. He was, in fact, known in our small community as "the soul of complacency." There's that word again, like so many others shedding great chunks of its meaning every time it recurs. Poor soul. Poor Father. Poor me.

4. He did not do sports. He did not even watch sports. He said to me once, when I pleaded to be taken to a baseball game, that he did not see the sense of sports, particularly baseball. What was the point, he asked, of playing a baseball game one day and then having to go out and play another game the next day? Year in and year out? And grown men, besides? What did you ever get accomplished like that? Those were difficult questions for a child to respond to, and often, in the years since, sitting in the ball park on a hot Sunday afternoon watching the second game of a long doubleheader, I have still wondered about them.

5. He read books, but he did not watch movies or tv. Perhaps the flickering screens of the visual media, so many frames per second and all that, were out of synch with his own internal scanning mechanism, so that in fact he saw nothing on those screens. Books, however, he read rapidly and in great number. Whenever he got to the end of a book, he looked up and said, "That was a good book." Then he laid it aside and picked up another. Once, as a teenager, I attempted to test him by asking him what the book he had just finished reading was about, but all he said was, "Read it and find out for yourself."

## To Be or Not To Be

\*     \*     \*     \*     \*

Evidence against the android theory:

1. He married, he fathered a child, he performs all the usual bio-
logical functions of a human being, he is even aging. On the
other hand, could not a clever android have been programmed
to do all these things? What do I know of what goes on behind
closed doors? Was I there at my own conception, any more than
anyone else? Is *conception* even the right word for how I came
to be? Or is it too, like *soul*, gradually losing its meaning? And
would not androids too, just like words, grow obsolete as the
state of the art progressed and have to be readied for the discard pile?

2. When I visited him at his retirement home after the first time
my wife threw out that accusatory term—though before she had
applied it to me—I asked him what he knew about androids.
He claimed he had never heard the word before. "Never heard
of androids?" I challenged. "Hemorrhoids?" he said. "Of course
I've heard of hemorrhoids; why don't you speak clearly?" I have
never known him to be sick, but he did occasionally suffer from
hemorrhoids. It would be just like them to have given him some
minor human discomfort, nothing disabling, just a petty irri-
tant, a humbling little flaw lest he ever begin to question his
android perfection. And at the same time they might well have
denied him the whole concept of *android*. He could not consider
what his programming would not even let him conceive of. That
was their master stroke. Never, never even for a moment, could
he be a victim of self-doubt.

3. Other people. No one, none of his business associates or social
acquaintances, none of the other retirement home residents,
not his doctor or dentist or accountant, has ever suggested to
me that he might be an android. Is it possible that none of them,
either, is familiar with that word? Is there anywhere that words
are working properly anymore? And his family! How could I
have forgotten that he has a family, brothers and sisters and
cousins? That he too once had parents? How could there be
such a thing as an android family? Isn't that almost a contradiction in terms? What does that mean exactly, "a contradiction in
terms"? Of course, as people have often remarked to me, he
and his brothers and sisters and cousins are all very much alike,

and not just in personal appearance. Even now, in my middle
years, when I run into aging acquaintances of his on the streets
or in the supermarket, they say, "Oh, I know whose boy you
are." Surely there cannot be such a far-flung conspiracy of androids as it would take to account for all of this. True, my father
and his peers all live on into healthy old age; many of them
take up residence finally at the same retirement home, but isn't
that just a benefit of the advanced state of our society, of good
medical care and improved nutrition, simply what is reflected
in the national statistics on longevity? Of course, this whole
group is factored into those very statistics. They account for
themselves. What does it prove? Am I to believe that the retirement home is also attended by android doctors and android
morticians, programmed like my father himself not to be cog-
nizant of androidism when they come to care for the "sick" and
to remove the "dead" and prepare them for "burial"? Am I to
believe that an android such as my father will ever truly "die"?
What am I to believe? What am I to believe?

\*     \*     \*     \*     \*

I am not really interested in the social and political ramifi-
cations of this question. I do not even care if there is a "far-
flung conspiracy of androids" as I myself have already imagined. Is a conspiracy of androids even possible? Are not androids merely tools, like hacksaws and pipe wrenches, that
do what they were designed to do? You cannot have a conspiracy of hacksaws and pipe wrenches, can you? But you
could have a conspiracy of plumbers. You could have a conspiracy of the masters of the androids. But who are they?
Where are they? See how quickly things begin to slip away
from you once you begin to think like that! I am not interested in pursuing the android question into the mists of infinite regression, infinite paranoia. I do not care if the whole
world is run by androids. I only want to know one thing, one
simple thing.

Am I or am I not an android?

\*     \*     \*     \*     \*

Some might say that that is not a truly serious question,
that it is not even a healthy question, that it is the question

of a sick mind obsessed with its own condition and is therefore in itself, since no android would be programmed with
such a fruitless and distracting obsession, clear evidence that
I am not an android. It is, they would say, a self-dismissing
question. But I cannot seem to dismiss it. No matter how hu-
manly my children push their toy cars between my feet and
climb up onto my lap and call me "Daddy," I cannot dismiss
it. Poor little children, what do they know of their condition?
No matter how much I tingle all over when my wife touches
me in certain ways and whispers into my ear certain things
only a truly inhuman creature would be callous enough to
write down for others to see. Who would have projected even
an android into such a fleshly, human world as this and denied it the simple pleasures of sex? Surely not even the masters of the androids, no matter how nefarious the aims of
their conspiracy, would have been so cruel as that. Surely not
even a god would have been so cruel as that.

And regardless of what others might say, it still remains a
serious question for *me*. At least according to my own sense
of what constitutes a serious question, which is to say that it
is a question that makes a difference. To others, excepting
perhaps my wife, it is not a serious question, because to them
it makes no difference whether I am an android or a human
being. One way or another, I drink my Scotch with them and
go to the symphony with them. I do my job and clothe my
children decently and rake my yard. I am up on the news.
They see me at church. They know I have made an effort to
take up golf, even if I have not managed to stick with it. They
admire the late-model cars that I always drive and how I always keep them in immaculate condition. They find my wife
and myself an amiable couple. What more could they want
of me? To them, an amiable android is just as good as an
amiable human being. Why should the question of my android condition ever arise? Surely they would find it as gauche
as asking whether there was Jewish blood in my family background.

I suppose I should be thankful to be taken at face value like
that, not to be plagued by all the niceties of discrimination,

not to have to wonder if my children are being allowed to play with their children out of sympathy or if I myself am being condescended to every time I am invited over for a drink. Not to wonder if they are smiling, out in their kitchens where they are mixing the drinks, about my upward mobility—as if I could ever actually be human, like them—and puzzling over what to do if I decide to apply for membership in the country club.

It is good, I suppose, to be spared that, if indeed I am being spared that, for how would I know what goes on out in their kitchens? But however it does or does not affect them, it is still an important question for me. It makes a difference for me whether I am an android or not, because, quite simply, if I am an android, I do not have to think, any longer, about what I do, what I am. If I am an android, there is nothing else I can do except to do what I do. What I am programmed to do. Am I programmed to do *this*? If I am an android, there is no point whatsoever in thinking about it. There is no point in anything except getting on with it. There is no point even in thinking about whether I am an android or a human being, because no matter how much I think about it, I am still going to remain an android.

If I am not an android, however, then I have got to think very carefully about what I am doing, because whatever it is I am doing, it is not my programming doing it, but I. And what is this *I*? Is that a valid term for me, an *I*? That is the other thing I have got to think about if I am not an android. If I am not an android, I have got to think about what it is for this *I* to be human. If I am not an android, then whatever this *I* is, is up to me.

See what a difference it makes!

If it seems like it must be a hard thing to be an android in a human world—and I am sure that is a very hard thing indeed—still, it is beginning to look to me like it is a harder thing by far to be a human being in any sort of world.

But how am I ever to know which I am?

Who will help me?

## To Be or Not To Be

\*      \*      \*      \*      \*

Not my wife, who, it seems, has already made up her mind
on the issue, who has stormed off upstairs to the bedroom
screaming, and then grown suddenly quiet, at least leaving
me a certain peace in which to consider these issues. But how
will we ever resolve our differences if she is upstairs screaming and sulking while I am downstairs thinking and thinking? It would be nice to settle something before the children
come home from roller-skating and insist on showing us what
it was like, spinning around and around in the middle of the
living room until they fall to the floor, hysterical and dizzy
and exhausted. Such chaos then! Nothing can be resolved
like that. And it is hard to leave things unresolved, one of the
hardest things about living with a human being.

"Another human being," I was about to say, but I no longer
know if I have a right to say that.

I suppose I could simply follow her upstairs, now that there
has been a brief cooling-off period, and attempt to make peace
with her. It has been done before. I could ignore the issue
and simply apologize for my part in the hostilities. That would
surely be easy to do. What harm could there be in that? The
issue must have been trivial anyway, as the issues always are.
I no longer even remember what it was. But even though the
issues fade, the charges remain. Things have been said, and
what do they mean? Can we ever truly know? We have
plunged into each other too deeply, as always, and how can
that ever be resolved? Upstairs, of course, there is also the
bed, where we know how these penetrations can be resolved, and with what mutual satisfaction. But will even that
work any longer, I wonder. Or will I be thinking, all the while,
what must it have been like for her to have been making love
with an android all these years?

When did she first suspect it?

First know for certain?

And why has she waited so long to tell me?

\*      \*      \*      \*      \*

The first thing I thought after she stalked away was how unsatisfactory I found the conclusion of our argument to be. Was there, I wondered, hope in such dissatisfaction? I hoped so. If I were an android, after all, would I not have been satisfied simply to have stuck to my logical guns? After some time, I sat down on the couch and turned on the television and tried to watch it for a while to distract myself from all these disturbing thoughts that had swept over me in the wake of our argument. But I could not seem to concentrate on the tv; I could not even have said what I was watching. What, exactly, was the source of my dissatisfaction? The terms of our argument, I recalled, had remained reasonably clear throughout, and, at the end, I had even persuaded my opponent to see the logical alternatives of her position. At which point she departed. I saw from the *TV Guide* that there was a baseball game on the other channel, but I didn't feel like getting up to switch it over. How could such an argument have been both proper and utterly dissatisfying? So perfect in form and so muddled in outcome? Was it possible there was another category we had not considered, the half-human, half-android? Was such a mixed breed possible, and, if so, was that the sort of mongrel I myself was? How would one ever know exactly what one was if that was the case? The thought made me somewhat queasy. In what direction could one even begin to proceed with such a notion as that? It seemed like even more vertiginous territory than that I had already been exploring. Instead, I picked up the library book my wife had left lying on the end table beside the couch. Considerable time must have then passed. The room had grown quite dark. My wife had returned and was standing in front of me, looking greatly calmed. I was just finishing the book. I closed the covers and placed it back on the end table.

"I've been meaning to get to that book myself," she said. "How was it?"

"Why don't you read it," I said, "and find out for yourself."

# Disorder and Belated Sorrow: A Shadow Play

When I moved out, I left a dark persona behind me, a creature who used to wander the house at all sorts of odd hours, closing cabinets, emptying wastebaskets, checking the locks on doors, a demon of tidiness and security. Not cleanliness: he could live with a surprising amount of dirt. He recognized the world's penchant for both dirt and disorder and chose which one he, personally, was going to do battle with: let the dust collect, it was his task to straighten the pile of magazines on the coffee table, untangle the telephone cord. If he devoted a morning to doing the laundry, his aim was never to cleanse the dirty clothes but only to banish the messiness of the laundry basket, to conceal its tangled confusion within the white cubes of washer and dryer, to hurry socks and underwear back to the neatness of dresser drawers. And he was good at it: you should have seen him in the kitchen!

With people, however, it was a different matter. He spent the whole day looking forward to their reappearance—those shining, touchable creatures who shared the world he tried to make *just so*—but fearful of the confusions they brought back with them. Better they should come home dirty, there was no worry in that realm for him, but packed to the brim with disorder, bubbling over with disorder, sloshing disorder here in the living room, there in the kitchen, that was more than he could deal with. Oh, it was what he *wanted* to deal with, but more than he could. Especially when he saw these overflowing vessels convinced that what they overflowed with was order itself. The problem was that when he heard them say—in response to his own humble request, of course: Look, please, I'd appreciate your not making such a mess—that they weren't chaos, that they were order itself, whether he could see it or not, not *his* sad excuse for order but order all the same, why, he believed them, after a fashion. He took the world—the word—at face value, and if the word was order, he took it as order, though often enough he was soon left on his own with the fact that it sure didn't *feel* like order. So that even when something that passed for whatever order was to him was at last achieved on the outside, he was still left with this confusion between what the world said and what he felt, between the word and the thing, on the inside. This disorder. And there were no drawers it could be tucked away in—he was smart enough to know *that*—unless he was willing to look on himself as a drawer, which he wasn't, especially for what he looked upon as other people's messes. Apparently he wasn't smart enough to know better than *that*.

There are times when I want to go back and visit him— back where I used to live and he, somehow, still does (though I'm not altogether sure he would welcome me in)—in order to say to him: Look, there are no other people's messes. Where you live there is only your own mess. Isn't that *enough* confusion for you? But I'm certain he knew that all along, and surely he doesn't need to hear it from me at this late date; I could probably knock all afternoon at his door and get no answer, call him up only to have my identity questioned. He was always a great one for confronting the validity of other people's categories, knocking over their small attempts at putting things in piles, even with that other persona he shared the house in wry oxymoron with, his female alter ego, contrary appositive, seeker extraordinaire to his settled ordinary.

Here she is, for example, having just arrived home in what used to be described as a state of great dishabille. Her blouse is only partially tucked into her skirt, the skirt itself twisted halfway around, her straight and usually neatly combed brown hair all atangle, and a small bruise darkening on her left cheekbone.

"Albert, Albert," she exclaims, "I've found it at last. After all these years at the edge, I've finally made the leap, no, I didn't leap, I was pushed, and listen to this, you'll never guess what it was that pushed me, but I'll tell you, it was mysticism, it was mysticism that pushed me. After all these years! I was just standing at the edge as usual and along came mysticism and pushed me over and I fell—no I didn't fall, it was more like I went up. I was raised. Lifted. I soared, glided. I flew! It was everything, everything I ever looked for, everything I always knew it could be, one, all. And listen, this may be the most important part: it wasn't Eastern mysticism that did it, not Zen, not even Emerson you know, but good old Western mysticism, the mysticism of the priests and rabbis, the mysticism of . . . I don't know. The mysticism. *Mysticism* mysticism!"

Albert, Albert takes in this disarray of language and appearance from a sitting position in his favorite living room chair, the genuine leather one, Rob Roy in hand. "Zena," he inserts quietly into her first pause, "mysticism is not enough."

"Listen, dummy," she says, kicking off her shoes and squatting down in front of him, "that's what you said when I was into rationalism back in the sixties. I came home very prim and solemn and sat down across the table from you and told you, very clearly and in great detail, everything I'd just found out about empiricism and inductive and deductive reasoning and all the rest of that rationalistic crap, and then when I was finished, while we were eating dessert—raspberry Jello with pineapple slices, my god, I remember the whole dinner, I made beef stroganoff, I came home and went into the kitchen and cooked a complete meal—wasn't *that* rational!—before I even began to talk to you about the most exciting thing I'd ever learned. Anyway, as soon as I was finished, right in the middle of the Jello, you said, 'Zena, rationalism is not enough.'"

She stands up barefoot in the middle of the living room and mimics him, saying it over again in her deepest voice: "'Zena, rationalism is *not* enough.'"

I cull this indecisive incident from my massive collection of notes on his past behavior—all carefully cataloged and filed away, from *A* to *Z*, for future reference, in a certain four-drawer filing cabinet—only to indicate the inconsistency of this character who denies to others the right to tidy up their worlds that he applies to his own. If not terribly smart, he is at least crafty: he has devised a category that does not permit categorization. For use on other people, naturally. My desire to send him a postcard, one of my elegant National Gallery cards perhaps, maybe Holbein's *The Ambassadors*, with an unsigned, one-line message scrawled on it—Categorization is not enough—is only forestalled by my realization that, in spite of the fact that my card would have been unsigned, I will probably get a one-word message in the return mail, on a plain, post office postcard like as not: Precisely.

But like any such incident, this one proves nothing: neither that mysticism is not enough (because the *rationalist* says so?) nor that rationalism is not enough (not *even* because the rationalist says so: irony is not enough either). Nor, for that matter, that any such thing ever really happened (is imagination enough?). If it proves anything at all, it is only that, like all such incidents, it is perhaps capable of casting, by the light of its own dim fluorescence, a faint shadow—the shadow of a shadow, in fact—upon a background I have sketchily erected for it ("the house at all sorts of odd hours"), deliberately leaving it as plain, as uncluttered (where did that passion for tidiness come from?) as possible, in order that the shadow itself might be more clearly seen, moving across this curtain of the past ("I left . . . behind me").

And shadows move—if only because the source of light that gives them their life, their reality, moves, changing their shape and size and clarity of outline. The incident illuminates the shadow, the shadow illuminates . . . what?

I am often tempted to go back and find out what: even to ask it as a direct question, if need be. Back to the world where that "dark persona" of this shadow play haunts the kitchen, laundry room, toolshed, closets, drawers, master of reorganization, a blessing to have flitting about you in the kitchen while you cook, as he soundlessly slips the spices back into the spice cabinet, washes out the blender, the mixing bowls, the pots and pans and utensils you have used and laid aside, sponges off the counter tops . . . *voila!* The meal is done and the kitchen is immaculate! To eat is a joy in such surroundings, and quickly everyone sits down at the table, ready to

## Disorder and Belated Sorrow

dig in—fish curry tonight, rice, dahl, curried vegetables too—
when he looks around: whoever set the table left the silverware drawer halfway open, the telephone rings, the dog barks
his deep bark at the newsboy coming up the front walk to
make his monthly collection, one of the children begins to
complain about his food: "I don't like the taste of cooked tomatoes."

"Eat them," orders Zena at precisely the same moment that
Albert says, "So don't eat them then." So?

So nothing: as a shadow play no more illuminating than a
television situation comedy, to achieve which level of art it
yet needs two of the children to begin squabbling with each
other, Zena to answer the phone (her mother, long distance),
and Albert to get his foot tangled in the cord as he leaves the
table to answer the doorbell. But these things it shall not have.
Not here certainly. Too much clutter: perhaps they belong to
another incident, or none at all, but they would lead toward
the development of an overriding idea—Total Chaos—whereas
here there is no idea at all, only a smattering of ordinary disorder. It will not do to extract from this little incident—selected at random from an unlabeled file folder, sketched at
whim—the theme of the absurd universe, merely because, in
the midst of a little unexpected activity, the food has gotten
cold. It is the shadow we are interested in, not the act.

And the shadow is what shadows are: flat and dull, taken-
for-granted, two-dimensional, dependent, confined to life on
the surfaces of things—other things. Over those things he
moves, to be sure, fluidly enough, especially when lit by the
sunshine of daily life. And into them he quickly fades when
the dark night of anyone's soul turns down the lamps: for it
is those surrounding souls here—that wife, those children—
who illuminate him, who bring him to life—shadow life, of
course, but life all the same—far better than I ever can. They
are, in a terribly literal way, the light of his life.

But what and where, it might be asked, is the object against
which the light is thrown to cast this shadow?

Look around.

Imagination casts the only shadow here. Or maybe any-

**161**

where: as, with children, the light of their imaginings casts the shadow of the father on the wall of their existence, larger than life. And the shadow moves: dark, protective, swelling and shrinking in the glimmer of the child's own moods, and, yes, overshadowing, a pun on existence, a joke without depth. Depth is not enough. We know that because shadows have none, being all surface. No guts.

So how is this shadow to know anything of what lurks inside the human heart? Well, he has his opinions, like all the rest of us, always slowly arrived at, usually far too late to be of any use. And naturally he has a word for what lurks there, too, though far too generalized and reflective of his own state to be of much value. *Disorder*, what else? But as to his accuracy: I have sifted through reams of data since leaving him behind—when I lived in closer proximity to him, I was always so preoccupied with what he was *doing* that I never managed to see any of those activities as capable of conveying any further information about him than mere presence (is *presence* enough?)—and have to conclude that the evidence, as they say, weighs heavily against him. He is an ignorant shadow. Perhaps all shadows are ignorant, I wouldn't know (and if I ever do know for sure, it will probably be too late to do me any good), and maybe it is even in the nature of shadows to be ignorant, poor two-dimensional creatures that they are, projections of the wandering lights we throw out across the screen of the past to give them their reality.

Which is an all-too-easy trick. No mirrors. Watch: he comes to life in the west-facing bay window of the living room, arranging the potted plants on their stands. Two of the begonias are infested with insects, the big, white-haired cactus called *old man* is rotting, and the false aralia is shedding its leaves from overexposure to the light, but he is concerned with patterns of proportion and balance: one blighted begonia on either side of the flowering gloxinia. Surely symmetry isn't enough!

Various other figures flit back and forth across the darker half of the room behind him, all on their own journeys, none concerned with the particular quest for order he is engaged in at the moment, shadows just like him apparently. But look

## Disorder and Belated Sorrow

how they step aside as they pass to make room for one another! Do shadows do that? I have seen how shadows move,
my records are full of their motions: they pass easily across
one another as if they had no substance at all, and nothing is
touched by their passing. From the movements here, however, from the sudden pauses when two of these figures come
together—just because it is darker there in their half of the
room and they *look* like shadows in the darkness (I have lit it
very badly) does not make them shadows, not yet anyway—
from their awkward confrontations, their clumsiness in getting around each other in the doorway, the awkward sidestepping little dance they seem to do when they meet face to
face going in opposite directions, from the chaos of their coming together and the confusion of their attempts to make room
for one another, from their mutual presence, I conclude that
these are not shadows after all. They are real people, however dimly seen, they have real names (I do not have to go to
the file for that), and their disorganization, sad to say, is tes-
timony to their reality.

Can I take it then that my own disorganization—the fact
that I do not comprehend those awkward passages, no more
than I can make any sense of that dark persona more brightly
lit in the foreground, even though it is I and no one else who
has brought them forth here—testifies to my own reality? That
strikes me as terribly naive but nonetheless possible: *disorder
is enough*.

Not "sad to say," either: that must have been the voice of
the shadow speaking, his own misconceptions of the dismay
that lurks in the human heart. Lord knows I hear him often
enough. No, I do not really need to visit, phone, send post-
cards or telegrams, or look him up in my tedious archives, so
tightly packed that only something as thin as a shadow could
be slipped in among them. We are in constant communica-
tion: well, not altogether constant, but constantly available,
there, almost, but not quite, like genuine presence, only a
little too thin, a little too . . . intangible, given to gliding a
little too easily over surfaces without ever disturbing their
contents.

Therefore I *do* go back. Not merely to assure myself that he is still there, wandering transparently between the plant shelves and the kitchen, the laundry room and the attic storage bins, disorder swarming up in his wake like life: the shelves once devoted to literary criticism now contain books on psychology, gardening, poetry, East Asian politics; unmatched socks are brought forth regularly, helplessly, from the basement; the single mint plant gone wild ousts the sedum from the borders of the kitchen garden. But also to learn from the nature of his being there that perhaps—"perhaps," I say: just a moment ago I thought I had this all neatly worked out, but suddenly I am no longer certain wherein that neatness lay— perhaps presence, without which there is nothing, of course, is not enough. It is a lot, because it is a way of being and not, like rationalism or mysticism or irony, a way of perceiving, but it is not, I think (Does the shadow concur? Yes, I think I will have even the shadow concur), quite enough, all by itself. It is too pure. A shadow: which cannot really *be* because it needs an equal purity of background on which to exist, and there are no pure backgrounds, excepting such artificial ones as I have constructed here in order that we might see the shadow *as* shadow. No, backgrounds are full of depth and motion and disparity, into all of which a shadow cast upon them quickly disappears.

And in that way, lost in the depths of that reality, the shadow play, like the shadow, comes to an end. Into that reality the wife, ex-wife, Zena, settles down with her book in the living room chair the shadow has vacated, sloshing onto its real leather some coffee out of the cup she balances awkwardly in her left hand. And the children, still children, settle down likewise to the evening's struggle with real math problems that wring from them cries of real anguish, thus:

"I can't do this! Won't someone help me?"

No answer. Shadows have ears, but they are shadow ears, with no connections to real, gutsy problems.

Even the dog settles down now beneath the round Formica kitchen table, down in the shadow cast by the table and the child sitting there doing her homework. Even the dog! Did I fail to give the dog his due before? Well, make it a huge dog, then, shaggy and aging, a Saint Bernard, if you will, shedding hair over everything and, when he swings his great head, splattering long strands of thick drool across the furniture, the walls, the paintings, where eventually, uncleaned, it hardens like cement. No wonder I tried to ignore the dog.

But only in such a reality as that, its slimy mess hardening slowly to concrete reality, ought this shadow play properly to end. Only when the shadow passes, plotless and ephemeral—lit by the weak bulb of memory in the hope of outlining some thin perceptions—and reality solidifies in its wake. Only then can both be taken for what they are. Enough, and not enough.

# Who Is This Man and What Is He Doing in My Life?

### 1.

I don't know. He is an oaf, a freak, an ungainly monster, a whoopee cushion on the overstuffed couch of my life. My therapist counsels me to ignore him and he'll go away, but my therapist is always of the opinion that I should ignore any problem I have and it will go away. I cannot deny that so far he has been right. For years he counseled me to ignore my mother, that she would go away, and he was right, she did, she died. He counseled me to ignore my wife, and eventually she went away also, leaving a costly divorce suit behind. Likewise he advised me to ignore that wretched beast of a dog I used to have, and finally it, too, ran away. There have been times when I thought that as soon as I left his office, after complaining for an hour of some problem, he was on the phone at once to that problem, telling him, her, it, to go away at once. Only I knew he wasn't that persuasive. I had spent quite enough time with him to know the limits of his effectiveness. This man will be the real test, though. This man is not like a mother or a wife or a dog. This man is not family. He does not know how to read my mind. If I ignore this man as successfully as I have ignored various others—other people, other problems—and still he does not go away, it will be time to consider changing therapists.

### 2.

The major problem is that he is too big. How can you ignore something this big? He fills the doorway. There is no room to get around him. He is like an onrushing planet in my personal *War of the Worlds*, growing larger each day, looming over all my horizons, filling all available space.

**166**

## Who Is This Man?

**3.**

He laughs when he announces that he could easily pick me up and toss me out the window. He laughs to let me know he is just making a joke. But he *could* easily pick me up and toss me out the window. It is no joke. He also laughs to show me he knows it is no joke. And I laugh with him, of course, in order to let him know that I know that he knows it is no joke. Ha ha. Ha ha ha ha. People tell me how much they like to see the two of us together because we are always having such a good time.

**4.**

Last Tuesday he picked me up early in the morning so that we could get to the amusement park as soon as it opened, so we could be the first ones there and have the roller coaster all to ourselves. I heard him honk and looked out the window to see him waiting at the curb for me in his yellow Buick convertible. He had the top down and was sitting up very erect in the driver's seat, his left arm hanging out of sight over the edge of the rolled-down window. I could imagine his knuckles scraping the asphalt. He is not ashamed of his size. Sitting up straight like that, he made the convertible look like a toy car. I hurried out before he had to honk again and climbed quickly up onto the front seat beside him, not quite knowing what to do with my legs because of the enormous distance between the seat and the dashboard. I just let them stick out in front of me. I asked him to turn the radio on, but he didn't. He didn't say he wouldn't turn the radio on; he just didn't do it.

**5.**

He is not very good to look at. I am a rather exceptionally good-looking man myself, no giant of course, a little on the small-boned side if anything, but with all the delicacy of features that goes with such a build, and I am often quite simply amazed, when I look in the mirror, to see the incredibly handsome creature who stares back at me there. At times it occurs to me that I am so exceptionally handsome that I ought to be someone other than who I am. Nonetheless, whenever we are together, he is the one whom people stare at. He with his coarse facial features and huge red hands, he with his ill-shaved beard and the tufts of black hair springing from his ears and nostrils. I am embarrassed for him, the way people stare at him, and I feel sorry for him when he returns their stares with his wide, innocent smile. I am not ashamed, then, to let him drape his heavy arm over my shoulders as we walk together.

6.

I have never known anyone else to enjoy the roller coaster so thoroughly. For myself, it has little more effect on me than any of the other silly rides in the amusement park, neither thrill nor terror, only, of course, that brief moment of apprehension as it crests the peak at the top of its first long, slow climb. But for him every moment of the ride is filled with joy. He rides the car, empty except for us, to the top of that first hill like some enormous jockey urging his horse to the front of the pack, bouncing up and down in his seat, whipping the side of the car with his meaty hand: thunk, thunk. We are sitting in the very front seat, and he has his other arm wrapped around my shoulders while I grip the metal bar in front of me with both hands. Then we plunge over the crest, gathering speed rapidly, and he rises from his seat, hanging onto the rail in front of us with one hand, waving the other in the air over his head, bellowing wildly at the top of his lungs. With the roar of the wind and the rushing car, the clamor of metal rails in my ears, I cannot make out what he is screaming. At times it seems that his great weight, standing and swaying as we sail over the sudden rises and clatter wildly around the curves, will unbalance the car, tip it over and off the track, and send us spilling down through the flimsy-looking wooden scaffolding to shatter on the concrete below. Only when we glide to a halt flush against the side of the loading platform does he slump back down into his seat and fall silent. I reach into my pocket for my wallet so that we can ride again.

7.

I often fail to understand what he is saying. Usually when that happens I just nod, and for the most part that seems to satisfy him. Sometimes, however, when he seems to require a more elaborate response, he looks down at me quizzically when I nod, knitting his heavy, dark brows, and speaks again. I assume on such occasions that he is repeating what he just said, but since I have not understood him the first time, I cannot be certain of that. His voice descends upon me from such a great height that usually I cannot understand him this second time either, and so have to ask him to repeat himself once more. I usually find myself taking a step or two backward when I make this request. It is clear to me that such an incident as this could easily result in his living up to his threat of picking me up and tossing me out the window, but generally he just shrugs. His voice is heavy but muffled, unclear, resonant, fuzzy, as if he were speaking loudly but from the chamber of a deep cavern. Often, too, as on the roller coaster, he will turn to address himself to me just as some other sound is rising to overwhelm us. He sits erect and silent in his convertible all the way home from the amusement park, gripping the tiny steering wheel in his paws, only turning to speak to me when we enter the roar of freeway traffic, when we plunge into the echo chamber of the downtown tunnel, when diesel semis are passing us on both sides. He leans over toward me as we roar through the tunnel, diesels thundering away on both sides of us, and reaches out with one hand to flick on the radio as he opens his mouth to speak to me.

8.

My therapist, who sees me as a stronger, larger person than I really am, remains adamant. But look at me, I tell him, do I look like a man prone to physical violence? The delicate bone of my nose would shatter like the stem of a crystal wine glass. He has me confused with some other patient, I tell him. Nonsense, he says. He insists he was only talking about inner strength, the strength to refrain from physical violence if anything, the strength to ignore whatever seems inappropriate or displeasing, the strength to turn the other cheek. My cheekbones! I exclaim. Like china teacups!

9.

My friends like him. In fact, they seem to me to be rather overly fond of him. At Pauline's party they absolutely surrounded him with their goodwill, they flowed like the incoming tide across the living room toward the corner where he leaned heavily against the wall, they lapped up against the great promontory of his presence like dancing, sunlit waves. The cup of coffee he held in his hands looked like it belonged to a dollhouse tea set. From across the room it is apparent that they are merely being condescending to him. Their condescension splashes against the dark cliffs of his ignorance and sends up a fine spray of laughter. He laughs with them, opening his wide mouth to show the great gaps of missing teeth like caverns eroded by the sea. He is saying something as he laughs, but I can't understand it, though it makes the rest of them, swirling about him, laugh harder still. Pauline is carrying the coffeepot in from the dining room to freshen his cup. John stands back as she approaches to open a passage for her. That's right, that's right, I can hear John crying in his high voice. But I can't tell whether he's talking to him or to Pauline.

10.

The next afternoon Hank came over. As soon as she came in, I had the distinct feeling she wanted to talk to me about something that had gone on at the party, specifically about something that was passing, unspoken perhaps, between him and Pauline. But he was there at the time. We had just come back from the beach, and he had been hungry. He hadn't said anything; he had just taken the house keys from my hand as I got out of the car and gone up the walk ahead of me and let himself into the house. It was hard to keep pace when the mood struck him to move on like that. He left the keys dangling from the lock in the front door. When I got into the house, I found him in the kitchen making some ham sandwiches. That's where we still were when Hank arrived. I could see at once that she wasn't going to be able to talk to me about what she had on her mind, so we just stood in the kitchen watching him eat his ham sandwiches. After a while, seeing how she was staring at him, I asked Hank if she wanted a ham sandwich, too. No, she said.

## 11.

I had not exactly had a terrific time at the beach, discovering what it is to be submerged in the shade of another person. I do not mean the shadow of another figure falling casually across your body where you lie stretched out on your beach towel on the sand, a familiar enough phenomenon surely, only warranting a momentary glance upward to see an anonymous figure passing between you and the sun, balancing an armload of ice-cream sandwiches and root beer. I mean the shade, not the shadow. To have him lower himself slowly down beside me on the beach, where he did not even bother to spread a blanket out beneath his body, was to be plunged into a dense shade, as if the midday sun had suddenly set behind the cliffs that edged the beach. There were no cliffs. Abruptly the air grew still and dark and cool. It was no longer possible to wear my sunglasses if I wanted to see anything at all. It was as if we were in the midst of a sudden and unpredicted eclipse, and I dared not look upward into that enormous darkness where the sun was supposed to be for fear of doing permanent damage to my retinas. Instead, I lay face downward in the shade. Possibly others passing by envied me my protection from the sun, for it was a blistering hot day, but where I lay, a great chill fell over me and it was too dark to read.

12.

He first arrived not long after that beastly huge dog of mine had run away. He simply stood there filling my doorway, blocking sun and sky even on that first occasion, and wearing around his neck one of those heavy, chain-link chokers that had been fashionable a season or two earlier. Nothing else about him was even that remotely in style, though when I thought about his apparel later, I could see that it would be no easy matter for a man of his dimensions to carry off the latest styles with any flair, even if he could find things in his size. I had assumed at first, not being accustomed to having strangers appear at my front door, that he had come to tell me something about my dog, and though I dreaded the possibility of having that loathsome creature on the premises again, I was at the same time rather gleefully framing a witty remark to my therapist regarding the demise of *his* most cherished premise. The man whose huge frame filled my entire doorway had nothing to say about my dog, however. He did rumble out something, but I failed to catch what it was. Pardon me? I said, looking up at him. Because he had the sun behind him, I couldn't make out his features clearly. Everything about him except his size seemed somewhat obscure. He didn't repeat his initial statement, but instead took one step forward, which carried him well across the threshold, and stood there staring about the room. I, of course, had to back off several steps in the face of his entry. It soon became evident to me as I stood there before him, looking up into the vague, heavy features of his face, seeing how his own gaze roamed out over my head and around the living room, that this man had nothing to tell me about my runaway dog. At first I felt relieved, but close upon that followed a fresh surge of panic. Now what? I thought. What is this now? There is only so much that even a patient man like myself can be expected to ignore.

13.

Now John drops by to explain why they are inviting him to go out dining and dancing with them this weekend and not me. It's nearly noon, and I invite John to come in and have lunch with me. We'll fix ham sandwiches, I suggest to him, and talk about this a little. When I look in the refrigerator, however, I find that there is no ham left, only a plate with a bare bone on it. Never mind, I tell John, we'll find something. While I stand at the counter chopping celery and onions for the tuna-fish-salad sandwiches, I try to put John at ease by assuring him that I am not at all upset by the news he has brought—Believe me, I tell him, it's all for the best, he and I have been spending far too much time together. John remains silent while I open and drain the can of tuna, mix in the mayonnaise. Then he says, Do you have any whole wheat bread? I set our two sandwiches on the kitchen table, each one sliced carefully on the diagonal; then I go to the refrigerator and take out two bottles of beer and set them down beside our plates. I twist the cap off mine and take a quick, cool swig. John looks at me over the sandwich half he holds in his hand. No thanks, he says politely, none for me. I am dumbfounded. I am still holding my own bottle of beer in my hand, ready to take another drink. I have never in all these years seen John turn down a beer, especially an ice-cold beer with a tuna-salad sandwich on a hot summer afternoon. We're not drinking any more, John says.

14.

Although I threatened to call the police off and on during the course of his next several visits, a month or so might have passed before I actually did so. I was trying, among other things, to be a good patient, to develop the personal growth and mature sense of stability and self-reliance my therapist had promised he was guiding me toward. To do so, however, I felt that it was becoming necessary to reclaim some of the privacy with which the departures of my mother, my wife, and my dog had blessed me. Though I might not be possessed of the size, strength, and courage with which my therapist seems all too eager to credit me, I am not lacking in a certain determination and readiness to act in accord with my own needs, within limits. As usual, he stood a step or two inside the front door—his steps, that is, five or six of mine—his close-cropped head brushing the ceiling, saying nothing, watching me dial. When I was finished talking he came over to the telephone table, snapped the cord between his thumb and forefinger, and with the other hand squeezed the instrument itself into a compressed mass of wire and plastic. Then he crossed the room and sat down on the couch. When the two police officers arrived, both burly young fellows I was happy to see, they stood opposite the couch, right at eye level with him, facing him across the little coffee table, sizing him up. He smiled at them, friendly, open-mouthed. My god, I heard one of the policemen say, looking into that great, dark, open maw. Well? I said. I was standing a good ways behind them, in the dining room archway, beside the demolished telephone. The other officer stepped around the coffee table to where he sat and reached out to feel the muscle in his arm. How ya doin', big fella? said the policeman. His hand looked like a child's against that massive upper arm. Then he whistled, wheet wheew. The other policeman whistled, too, the same whistle. Then they both started out the door. Well? I said from back by the telephone, a little more insistently this time. Sorry ta trouble ya, said the one who had whistled first. The other just waved goodbye and pulled the door shut behind him.

15.


Pauline's friend, Thelma, whom I've always been attracted to, stops by in the evening. She flips the unlocked screen door open and barges right in without bothering to knock. I haven't been locking the doors, anyway, since the day he was too impatient to wait for me to get my keys out. Christ, says Thelma, why don't you get your telephone fixed, we've been trying to call you for weeks, all we get's a recording saying it's out of order, hey, what happened to your tv set, Jesus, look at that, will you. And your couch!

## Who Is This Man?

## 16.

The opera was my idea. If it has to be, it has to be, I thought, but it doesn't have to be just one endless roller coaster ride. Ignoring didn't always have to mean just closing your eyes to something; it could also mean looking for some distractions, as I pointed out to my therapist. He absolutely beamed. The Met was in town, sold out months in advance as always, but the usual standing room was available, and I presumed that might be best for us anyway. Appropriate dress was also something that had to be ignored, but, I thought, let the opera itself be the distraction from that particular dilemma. We stood deep in the darkness at the rear of the hall, gripping the brass rail that topped the low wooden wall behind the last row of seats, just as if we were clutching the bar at the front of the roller coaster. The sound in that hall is remarkable; wherever you are, it seems to well up right around you. I have never enjoyed Wagner more; I felt as if I were in the very midst of it. At intermission Pauline and Frederick, coming out the center aisle, spotted me in the shadows at the rear of the hall and came over at once. Have you been back here all along? Pauline asked: What was that awful sound coming out of the back here? Never heard anything quite like it, Frederick mumbled. What sound was that, I started to say to them, but then I could see that neither of them was paying any attention to me. They were both looking to my left and up into the higher shadows. My god, said Pauline. I stuttered something I thought might pass, with luck, as an introduction. Yes, of course, Frederick mumbled. He started to extend his right hand out and up but then withdrew it awkwardly as if he couldn't quite see where to place it. An unprecedented lapse of manners like that was something he was bound to hear about from Pauline when they got home later. Meanwhile, she had turned back to me to inquire whether I'd received the invitation to her dinner party. I was afraid I hadn't, not yet. Oh, she said, well it must be in the mail, then, I'm sure it will reach you in a day or so. Thank you, I said, it will be a real pleasure. Pauline is a wonderful hostess. But I wasn't sure she heard me; she was staring up into the shadows again. But you must attend to what the invitation says, she was saying, you must bring a guest, and it must be someone who has not been to one of my dinners before, you understand, you simply *must*.

17.

In my opinion John's letter goes rather overboard in its accusations, though he claims to have checked with Pauline and Frederick and Ralph and Norton and several others, unnamed, and to have found them all in essential agreement. Essential agreement, I suspect, might allow a little leeway that isn't altogether accounted for in the tone of the letter, which levels its charges with the full weight of consensus. Nonetheless, it is quite clear with whom their true concern lies. That even in my own kitchen I failed to attend properly and seriously to what was being said, failed to learn. Continuing to gulp at my bottle of beer, for example, until it was empty. That I continue to do everything in my power to undermine his confidence. Failing to articulate my introductions, for example. That my behavior epitomizes a failure of the trust that is an absolute prerequisite for true friendship. For example, calling the police. That my visits to the amusement park, the beach, the zoo, the planetarium are not carried out in a real spirit of mutual joy. John understands that I have begun writing about him and demands to see this manuscript before further harm is done. At the end of the letter I am left wondering if the crisis between Pauline and Frederick, which, as I can tell from the postmark, only erupted after this letter was mailed, will soften John's judgment of me. Then I note in a PS that John is enclosing a second copy of this letter, a carbon, for him.

18.

At the zoo they refused to let us board the monorail that traverses the open-air displays of animals in their natural habitats. Weight distribution, they explained, refunding our ticket money and sending us back down the up stairway.

176

## Who Is This Man?

Families lined up waiting to board had to squeeze back against the walls to let us pass. Parents gripped children tightly by the arms, pressed them in behind their own bodies or turned the faces of the very young to the wall and then, when the children twisted their heads about to look up over their shoulders, reached out their hands to cover their eyes. Really! Parents simply have no idea what sorts of models they're setting for their children. At ground level I reached up and took one of his hands in both of mine, and we set off to see the animals as best we could on foot. His favorites were the antelopes, the wildebeest, and Thomson's gazelle, which we could only see in the distance, through the chain-link fence, as they romped about on their mock veldt beneath the steel pylons of the monorail. I would have expected him to prefer the hippo and the rhino, the great pachyderms, but no, he clung to the fence with both hands, his eyes focused on the distant ungulates, and would not leave until dusk, when it became impossible to see if anything was moving out there any longer. Earlier in the afternoon, when a piece of paper that had been protruding from his pocket all day fell out and sailed away on the wind, I chased it down and brought it back to him. It was the carbon of John's letter. But he would not let go of the fence to let me hand it to him, and, when I tried to stuff it back in his pocket, he reached down and slapped it away and held me for a moment, lifted me slightly off the ground with his hand around the back of my neck, so that I could not pursue it again. After it had blown out of sight, he set me gently down and released me and returned to his staring. In the evening, when we finally left, I could see, high up where he had been clinging to the fence all day, two holes in it, each big enough for a child to crawl through.

## 19.

You shouldn't have left early, Thelma told me as we sat on the floor in the middle of my living room. No kidding, she said, he was your responsibility, I don't care if you felt left out, when you went home it was your responsibility to take him with you, you brought him, didn't you? Jesus, she said, this tastes good, I haven't had a goddamned beer in I-don't-know-when. But you should have taken him home with you, she told me, Christ, you had no right to just go off and leave him behind like that, don't you know *any*thing?

20.

Even after he and Pauline moved into the new City Center high rise, he continued to come every day, but we tended to restrict our outings to the amusement park and the beaches. After a few visits we gave up going to the zoo; it seemed to make him too sad. And of course we couldn't go back to the planetarium after that first time. That was most unfortunate at the planetarium, but luckily the first two police officers to arrive were the same ones who had come to my house. His smile showed that he obviously remembered them, and the one officer just walked right over to him and reached up and gave him a little punch on the arm and said, Hey, big fella, how ya doin', remember me? The other officer stood back and looked around the place with his eyes wide and whistled, just like he had at my house, wheet wheew. Together they were very competent. There were no hard feelings, but clearly the planetarium was not a place for us to return to. The roller coaster was always the best, anyway.

21.

Look, I told my therapist, let's face it, it's not working. Wait a minute, he said, holding up his hand, just wait a minute now. Please, I said, don't let this upset you, I admire your approach, believe me, I'll bet you've never had a patient more thoroughly committed to it than me, in fact I'd be the first to admit it's been very successful in the past, but maybe it's just not appropriate in this situation, maybe you can't use the same approach to every problem, that's possible, isn't it? Wait a minute first, he said, are you sure you've really been using it right, are you sure you've really been ignoring him? That's exactly the problem I'm talking about, I told him, this is something it just isn't possible to ignore, why don't you come over and see for yourself. Oh, no, he said, just hold on a minute now, we can't do that, that's not the way it works, the way it works is we talk about your problems here and then you, not me, you understand, you, you go and deal with them out there, that's the way it works. Listen, I said, that's the whole point, it's not working. Are you *sure* you're ignoring him? he said. You can't ignore him, I told him. You've got to keep trying, he said, give it time. Time! I said: How much time? It's been months already! Oh, months, he scoffed, what's months, we're dealing with your whole life here, do you measure out your life in months?

22.

Several times a week now John stops by late in the afternoon, on his way home from work, to find me resting up after a long day on the roller coaster. Usually he finds me sitting in the living room with the front door left open for air but the shades drawn against the heat and light. I sit on the floor, leaning back against the remains of the couch, nursing my drink, a cool, water-soaked cloth lying beside me to wipe my sweaty face with from time to time. John sits down cross-legged on the floor opposite me. Naturally you understand, John tells me, that he only continues to come because of how important he knows it is for you. John tells me what a wonderful life he and Pauline have made for themselves, though there was apparently some difficulty when they first moved into the condo, especially about the elevator. Pauline's money soon took care of that. Hank may eventually move in with them, John understands. Pauline would do absolutely anything for him. They have wonderful plans. Of course Frederick still remains distressed. You didn't handle that well at all, John tells me. Me! I exclaim. I don't understand you, John says, don't you have any concept of how that man is feeling, how can you ignore your responsibilities like that? John, I ask him, what am I supposed to do, you can't have it both ways, can you, you can't blame me for holding him back and then blame me for letting him loose, can you? We're not talking about blame, says John, we're talking about responsibility, we're talking about people who think they can ignore their responsibilities. Hey John, I say, picking up the cloth to mop at my forehead, have a drink, huh, how about it? He shakes off my suggestion. Of course, he adds, there's no way Thelma can continue to see you under the circumstances. Hold on, I demand: Did *she* tell you to tell me that? If you ask me, says John, there's entirely too much focus on *your* feelings in the whole matter. My feelings! I cry: What have I got to do with it? Precisely, John says. He is really rolling along in high gear now. Do you realize, he demands, how much other people's lives are being governed by your feelings? He is practically shouting, his high voice scraping the very ceiling of the room. Do you know, he shrills, that he and Pauline are postponing their travel plans—all the wonderful travel plans they've made to Paris and Rio and Peking—just so he can continue to see you regularly, just so he can take you to the amusement park every day, even though riding the roller coaster fills him with fear and boredom, just so he can do anything, anything he possibly can, for you—where do you find friends like that, who will do absolutely anything for you? He scoots closer and closer across the floor toward me as he screams. I already have my back pressed against the shattered couch. Do you know? he shouts: Do you? Do you? I try to ignore him, but I can't.

# Not a Story by Isaac Bashevis Singer

One day, in a village so small and lost that it didn't even have a name, when Ronald was on his way home from the tailoring shop, alone, just as it was falling dark, he heard a voice speak to him out of a bush beside the road, telling him to go to America. It was very insistent.

"All right! All right!"

Ronald was a good young man, very obedient, always listening to what he was told, but in America no one spoke to him at all.

"Why is this?" said Ronald to the cracked mirror in his boardinghouse room. "I respect my parents and do everything they tell me, and what do they do but die on me. Like a slave I apply myself at the yeshiva, but one day the rabbi disappears and they will not send us another one. Zadie I bring flowers and solemn vows, and look where she is now. Living with a goy butcher. Not even married. I am in the shop stitching away even before the sun has risen, and what does the owner do when he comes in later stinking of tea and honey but cuff me on the ear.

"Now I come to America like I am told, and look what happens. I stand on the street corner greeting people in my best English, and they walk right by me without so much as a glance. I go into the tailoring shops to ask for a job, and they act as if I don't exist. Even when I offer to give them the first week for no wages, just to show what a good worker I am, they pretend not to hear me. Why is this?"

The reason for this was that they were not pretending. They actually did not hear Ronald. They did not see Ronald. To all of the world around him, Ronald simply didn't exist. On the boat to America they had never collected his ticket, though he had paid good money for it. In Europe it seemed he still existed. In Europe they took his money for the ticket. But here in America, nothing. His landlady, to whom Ronald thought he had explained his situation fully, did not even know there was anyone living in the top-floor garret. She still kept her sign in the front window, advertising the room to let. Ronald thought she had merely neglected to take it down.

Probably it was a good thing for Ronald that the mirror in which he was addressing himself was so badly cracked. If it had not been cracked, he too might have seen that there was no one there.

How did this come to be?

How did it happen that a personable young man like Ronald, sincere and hardworking, with the nimble fingers of a skilled tailor and such a gift for the English language you would have sworn he came over on the Mayflower, and not a bad fellow to look at either, if anyone could have seen him, had become such a nonperson? And in the famous land of opportunity besides, where he had been assured from his earliest childhood, when the whole family sat before the fire dreaming of going to America, that everyone was someone!

Who knows.

If this were a story by Isaac Bashevis Singer, we would know. Already this far into the story we would understand that Ronald had offended God, or even some minor spirit, and so had a lesson to learn. But Ronald offended no one. Ronald was always good. The best. He had some lessons to learn, why not? Everyone has lessons to learn. But not for punishment. Or it would be some mischievous golem that did it, like an emblem for the willfulness of the universe. Or some infernal incubus on a mission of vengeance, sucking Ronald's very identity away, leaving a silent, invisible shell behind. The sins of the fathers, et cetera, et cetera. Or one of those silly bets we hear about between God and the devil. How much can a man take? What man? Any man, that one over there, that Ronald. I don't know, let's see. But Ronald was no Job. Ronald was just Ronald. There were no bets. No incubi

## Not Isaac Bashevis Singer

or succubi or golems. No Isaac Bashevis Singer to rescue him from this dilemma. Just Ronald. It just happened.

To some people things like this happen.

Not to everyone, or how would all the business of the world ever get done, with nobody seen, nobody heard. But to anybody. Mr. Singer is a wonderful storyteller. The best. But the world is not a story by Mr. Singer, and therefore in the world a thing like this can happen. How? Poof! That's how. Just like that. One day. One day you get on a boat to America and nobody sees you anymore, nobody hears you anymore. You get to where you thought you wanted to be and you're nobody.

Ronald did not find this an easy way to live. No one paid any attention to him, but still he had an appetite, like any growing young man. For fear of starving, however, he had to abandon his landlady's boarding table, where there was never a chair or a plate for him, where no one would ever pass him a serving platter. In restaurants no one would wait on him. Other customers would rush in and grab his chair right out from under him, dumping him on the floor, into the sawdust, without so much as an "excuse me." In desperation he began to take things from the open shop windows on the street. First an apple. An orange. Then a banana. Ronald had never tasted a banana before. It was the first thing in all his days in America that gave him any pleasure. Soon he was taking whole bunches of bananas. No one noticed. He put them under his coat and carried them back to his room and ate them whenever he felt like it.

One day he saw a great hairy spider, bigger than his foot, crawling over one of the bunches of bananas in his room. Ronald was terrified. Such a spider as that, if it paid any attention to you, was worse than no one paying any attention to you, which was the worst thing that Ronald had known so far. The enormous spider crawled down off the banana stalk and across the room toward Ronald, who was too frightened to move, too frightened even to scream. Not that anyone would have heard him. The spider crawled right past Ronald and climbed up another stalk behind him and disappeared into a bunch of golden ripe bananas. Even the spider did not acknowledge Ronald's existence.

From that moment on, or at least as soon as he had stopped shaking from fear, Ronald understood his condition and knew that he was safe forever.

He could do whatever he wanted and no one would know. He did not have to just eat fresh fruits and vegetables from the shops; he could go into the kitchen right now and eat the leftover brisket. All he wanted. Naturally his landlady locked the kitchen at night, he had heard his fellow boarders complain of the fact, but for a mensch like him, what sort of problem was that? He could walk right into her room and help himself to the key. Like a common housebreaker. Only not so common, thanks to nobody could see him.

Already, no doubt, you're well ahead of things. With such a talent, why should he stop at a brisket, right? When he could help himself to a whole butcher shop. A jewelry store. A bank even.

True, true. Even to Ronald, virtuous, hardworking Ronald, who honored his mother and father and did whatever he was told, such thoughts occurred. He sat in the midst of his bananas and thought about Greenstein's store, where all day long the diamonds sparkled in the windows. From across the street was where he had always observed it, from his favorite fresh fruit stall, where the bananas were always firm and yellow, never full of dark, soft spots, though he didn't always take from there, that didn't seem fair. Now he pictured himself, for in his head he still had a good idea of what he looked like, standing in front of the bin of bananas looking across at Greenstein's windows, full of diamonds, which could in a flash be his. He was, he told himself, casing the joint. Listen to him! Like a hardened criminal he talks already! And how can they catch him? And what if they did? Where is the jail that could hold him? Where even the judge who could convict him? A judge should sit in his own courtroom passing sentence on an empty space? A laughing stock, that's what.

Now for the first time in your life, maybe, you are finding yourself on the side of the criminal. For Ronald's sake, you are willing to abandon a whole lifetime as a law-abiding citizen, maybe yourself the owner of a little shop just like the ones Ronald has been stealing fruit from. Yes, stealing! Just like the one he is mentally casing. Let him have his little revenge, you're thinking, on a society that won't pay him any attention, what can it hurt? Let him get a little something for all that neglect, which, poor fellow, he did nothing to deserve. Let him have his diamonds, if that's what makes him happy. At least that way there's a little justice in the world. Justice? That's justice? Well, you are probably reminding yourself, this isn't a story by Isaac Bashevis Singer, this is just the world, and in the world you have to take what you can get.

Ronald did not take Mr. Greenstein's diamonds.

So what kept him from this foolproof and undetectable life of crime? Neither the police of the City of New York nor the Talmudic studies that he still recalled. Not the mother to whom he promised on her deathbed that he would be a good boy all the days of his life. Not the innate honesty that shone from his face, back when his face could be seen, so clearly that the employer who beat him and who never let his own wife have a single coin sent Ronald to collect the bills. Not the slightest worry on Ronald's part that it was wrong, that it might cause hardship to others, that Someone might be watching, that he would pay for his crimes in the hereafter if not the here. None of that stuff.

The only thing that kept him from taking Mr. Greenstein's diamonds, and probably a whole lot more besides, was that he could not figure out what he wanted them for. What would he do with them? He could not give them as a token of his esteem to a young woman who could not see him. He could not sell them to someone who could not hear the ridiculously low price he was asking. And for what did he need money anyway, when no one could see him to take it from him, when he could take what he wanted without paying? Only there was nothing he wanted, except a little something to eat. Just a little, really, now that he was not so desperately hungry all the time. And maybe some day a new pair of shoes.

Well, there was one thing he could think of that he wanted.

He wanted to be somebody again, like he had been in the old country. Anybody, really. Anybody who could be seen and heard.

But he did not see how, even with his remarkable talent, which would allow him to come and go as he pleased, anywhere at all, even at Mrs. Rockefeller's, even at Mr. Vanderbilt's, he could steal for himself an identity. He sat on the floor of his room and ate another banana and told himself, first in English and then in Yiddish, that anything in the world was his for the taking, except the one thing he wanted. It sounded just as bad in one language as in the other. Then he looked through all the bunches of bananas for the spider, but he couldn't even find the spider anymore. Where could something as big as that spider have gone in this little room? he wondered.

The spider was not in his room any longer. The spider was downstairs, wandering about through the jungle of legs that were crowded together under the dining room table. No one was aware, yet, that the spider was there.

"Well," said Ronald, peeling himself another banana for consolation, "I guess this is just the way things work out sometimes. It happens. What can you do?" A good boy, that Ronald, not one to rail at his God, not one to weep and tear his hair and all that nonsense. But he could not eat his banana either. He just didn't feel hungry. He tried to stick it back in the bunch, then just let it fall to the floor.

From downstairs came a terrible scream, but Ronald didn't hear it.

From under the bed Ronald was busy pulling the little cardboard suitcase in which he had carried to America everything he owned. He blew the dust off. Ha, he thought, have I been here that long, that already I'm collecting dust? He threw in all his belongings. The rest of the space he filled with bananas. Then he started down the stairs. I will just stop by and say farewell to my landlady and my fellow boarders, he told himself, without thinking. But when he looked into the dining room, where everyone should have been at that hour, there was no one to be seen. Only the brisket sitting in the center of the table. When Ronald looked closer, for his landlady kept the gas lights as low as possible, he saw that it was not the brisket sitting there but the spider.

He wanted to say something to the spider before he left, but he didn't know what to say. He didn't even know if the spider could hear him. To be a spider, thought Ronald, that was really something. When you put in an appearance somewhere, people sat up and took notice. That was the life.

"Well," he finally said, when he couldn't think of anything else, "good luck. Even for a spider, life probably has its difficulties." The gas lights flared up for a moment, and the spider became a brisket again, and then, as the lights dimmed, a spider once more.

Whew, thought Ronald, what a world, never the same from one moment to the next, every day it seems to be getting more and more difficult to know what is what. But maybe that was just what life was like here in America, like his sudden invisibility, like everyone else's disappearance now. Were things that way in the old country, too? he wondered. He didn't think so. But then he remembered his parents and the rabbi and Zadie and thought maybe that was the way things always were and he was just now becoming aware of the fact. The world was just the world, a very shifty place. Only he himself was changing.

For better or worse, he thought, I am learning. After all, he told himself, this is not a story by Isaac Bashevis Singer, this is just life itself, in which anything whatsoever can happen, even to a poor immigrant boy from a village so small it has no name. Satisfied that he had arrived at a suitable conclusion, he pulled his cloth cap down on his forehead and bent over to pick up his cardboard suitcase. With his hand on its handle, however, he stopped, thinking, Who is this Isaac Bashevis Singer anyway? Then he hoisted the suitcase to his shoulder and went out the front door.